Praise for The Elevator

"*The Elevator* is a romance for the real world—Aria and Rob share a look and an attraction, but their lives are complicated, and connection doesn't come easy. The world doesn't pause for a look, though they—and we—wish it would. *The Elevator* is a warm, thoughtful, realistic novel of all the things that hold us back from love—everything from trauma and tough parents to bad timing—but also the kind friends, humour, and hamburgers that sustain us in the search for a partner. Love comes for Rob and Aria the way it does for most of us--in the middle of everything else."

— **Rebecca Rosenblum**, *These Days are Numbered, So Much Love*

"In *The Elevator*, Ramsingh crafts a poignant portrayal of the weariness of the modern dating world, steeped with missed opportunities, misguided intimacy, and a complex relationship with food. Brimming with vivid sensory details, Ramsingh centers a cast of characters both earnest and vulnerable in this engaging, compulsively readable story."

— **Deepa Rajagopalan**, Peacocks of Instagram

"Priya Ramsingh's superpower as a novelist is the ability to create authentic and empathetic characters. She did it with *Brown Girl in the Room* and now with *The Elevator*. I found myself rooting for Aria and Rob. I cringed as they tried to navigate the world of dating apps, agonized over bad dates and self doubt and then I eagerly awaited the next chance encounter."

— **Scott Colby**, Best-selling author and opinion page editor at the *Toronto Star*

The Elevator

Priya Ramsingh

The Elevator

a novel

Palimpsest Press
1171 Eastlawn Ave.
Windsor, Ontario. N8S 3J1
www.palimpsestpress.ca

Printed and bound in Canada
Cover layout and typography by Ellie Hastings
Illustrator (Aria): Jordan Sahay
Edited by Aimee Dunn
Copyedited by Sohini Ghose

Palimpsest Press would like to thank the Canada Council for the Arts and the Ontario Arts Council for their support of our publishing program. We also acknowledge the assistance of the Government of Ontario through the Ontario Book Publishing Tax Credit.

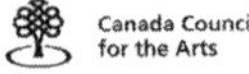

Canada

LIBRARY AND ARCHIVES CANADA CATALOGUING IN PUBLICATION

TITLE: The elevator : a novel / Priya Ramsingh.
NAMES: Ramsingh, Priya, 1968- author
IDENTIFIERS: Canadiana (print) 20240433416
Canadiana (ebook) 20240433572

ISBN 9781990293818 (SOFTCOVER)
ISBN 9781990293825 (EPUB)
SUBJECTS: LCGFT: Romance fiction.
CLASSIFICATION: LCC PS8635.A469 E44 2024 | DDC C813/.6—DC23

One

One of the elevators was broken. Again. Aria leaned against the wall and closed her eyes, tasting the staleness in her mouth—the kind that happens when the stomach is filled with air and nothing else. Hungry breath. She opened one eye and peeked at the buttons on the wall. The one she had pushed to go up was lit up in red, and upside down. Now both arrows pointed downward. Maybe it was a sign.

The miserable wait seemed in sync with the entire day. Aria closed her eyes and relived the incident between her coworkers. Lindsay, still upset at not getting the promotion she wanted, had kept mispronouncing Aman's name during the afternoon meeting.

Aman, who'd started a couple of weeks ago and got the job Lindsay wanted, said her name was short for Amandeep—a unisex Punjabi name, which made sense to Aria since the only other Amandeep she knew had been in her grade three class and had worn a Patka. Funny, how she couldn't picture his face—just the traditional Sikh head covering for boys.

Aria pushed aside the thoughts and shifted her focus to the highlight of her day, which was sitting inside a paper bag, clutched in her hand, brushing against her thigh, warm through the paper. Hopefully, it would stay that way until she got to her apartment on the seventeenth floor. Woody's burgers were the only ones she would allow herself to eat, and her last presentation of the day had been a short distance from the burger joint on the busy Lakeshore corner. It meant fighting through evening traffic but there was no way she could be close to the place and not stop in.

Besides, the kids had made her hungry. All of that talk about sweets and baked goods sent nags to her stomach. The presentation was intended to educate the students about proper oral health but ended with questions about foods they weren't supposed to eat. How many cookies were too many? Hotdogs—were they really bad? What about apple pie—wasn't it good because it had apples in it? Sometimes she wondered if she was the right person to be doing health promotion, given that she didn't really like talking about foods to avoid.

Over the past year, accepting food had been an uphill struggle for her. Walking directly to the bathroom after every meal was a pattern she couldn't remember being without. Often, she found herself standing in front of the toilet without knowing how or why she was there. Eventually, she learned how to revive a pleasant memory to take her mind off the food sitting in her bulging stomach right after a meal. Or to take a walk or even go out to her balcony for a change of scenery. They were all tactics learned from her therapist but it took time before Aria could bring herself to do these simple things. It took time before she would even admit that maybe the therapist was right.

But breaking that habit was all too easy. It only had to happen once. One slip, and a purge. It would be a relief not having to digest calories from a grease-laden burger. Ease the overnight worry that an inch would grow around her stomach, and push aside the plan of waking up early to go for a run on an empty stomach.

A swish of air grazed her face and Aria's eyes flickered to see the light-haired guy walk in through the door from the garage. He stopped about two feet from where she stood and her slump changed to a stand. The burger stop had made her later than usual. This was probably the time he got home every day. She recalled that he got off on the first floor in the mornings, and she figured that he was heading to the bus stop. Maybe he drove today.

His face was bent downward as he stared at his phone. She looked sideways, turning slightly to check out his hair. White. Blonde or grey? It was difficult to tell. He was tall—maybe six feet, and wearing a blue shirt and khaki pants; no tie. She couldn't remember seeing him in a tie before.

As she took a peek at his shoes, the elevator opened and the woman in the pink Coach hijab emerged, pushing her newborn in a stroller. The baby's brown eyes widened as she stared at Aria and a grin spread over the chubby face, exposing pink gums. The smile was contagious and Aria found herself grinning as she stepped into the elevator beside the light-haired man. Once inside the tiny space, she resisted the urge to look in one of the mirrors that lined the walls of the metal enclosure. She tucked a piece of her hair behind one ear, hoping the strands weren't fanned out on either side of her face from the static cling. The man pushed 14 as she had expected, and together they rode up, enveloped in the smell of grilled burger.

His floor came quickly. As the door opened, he moved to exit and she noticed a gym bag slung over one shoulder. Wait, was that a hesitation? His head turned slightly and she wondered if he was going to say something. Her mouth opened but shut quickly again. Hungry breath. He moved across the threshold and the door closed behind him. A surge of movement carried her up three flights to her apartment.

Aria didn't bother to change out of her work clothes. Instead, she lifted the burger from the brown paper bag and placed the wrapped sandwich onto a plate. It would get messy. She poured a glass of wine, took her meal over to the coffee table, and turned on the news. As she bit into the still-warm sandwich, the combination of grilled meat, melted cheese, and roasted-vegetable-mayo concoction took over her mouth and she sighed, feeling the gratitude from her rumbling stomach. She chewed slowly, savouring the taste, and looked at the television screen. A news reporter was standing in front of a school, talking about a Covid outbreak. The public health unit where she worked had been buzzing about it all day. She probably should have been paying attention to the news story but found herself tuning out. She'd had enough. She took a second bite, and as the flavours flooded her mouth once again, a sudden wave of guilt rushed through her. The chewing slowed. Aria stared at the screen and focused on the reporter, watching her mouth move while trying to listen but heard nothing. She continued to chew and chew until she allowed herself to swallow.

Aria had known about the burger joint for years, having heard about it from one of the girls at work. "They make them on site and throw them on the grill right after you order, so you have to wait," she was told. "But totally worth the wait and there are always cute guys standing around."

The thought was intriguing but she was only interested in the food and not the guys, since at the time, she was already dating Tyler. It was early in their relationship and although she knew he was a healthy eater, she figured that a burger now and then couldn't hurt. So, she mentioned it to him.

"Oh yeah, I've heard about that place." Tyler said. "Disgusting. Those burgers are slabs of fat, Aria."

It wasn't really the words but the tone of his voice that sliced through her. He'd looked right into her eyes at that moment, piercing her. She felt a surge of heat spread through her face and the moment froze as she watched his expression turn from disgust to mockery. It was the only time she had mentioned Woody's.

This particular evening, the place was jammed with men standing around in their suits or work boots and uniforms, eyes cast downward at their phones while burgers cooked and Drake droned overhead.

When she had walked in, eyes flew upward without heads moving, intending to stay discreet. Fingers stayed still and phones were momentarily forgotten while she ordered. While she wanted to smile at the guy in the plaid button-down shirt and jeans whose eyes she had caught while waiting, she didn't. Her stomach was nagging and she was conscious of her breath. What if he tried to talk to her? "A smile is an open door," Mila always said. Aria rolled the memory over in her head and took a sip of Cabernet, slightly stale from a bottle on its third uncorked day.

"How do you expect to meet someone if you can't even say hello?" Mila's voice rang in her ears. Usually, Aria didn't take kindly to judgements about her fears, but Mila was different. Somehow, her criticism was easier to take. "You're going to be single a long time if you can't open up."

"Right…one small break from men and suddenly I'm closed."

The same conversation had played out so many times that now Mila just rolled her eyes and changed the subject. She had no issues talking to men or women—whatever she felt like at the time. Since coming out as trans, Mila was still trying to figure out her sexuality, and Aria often envied her confidence.

But Mila had a good point. Aria should have initiated a conversation with the light-haired man by now. Two years of running into one another in the elevator and the most they'd done was exchange polite, neighbourly smiles. He was handsome in a waspy kind of way. Traditional, clean-cut Caucasian looks. Light hair, blue eyes, button-down shirts with starched collars, and reasonable shoes—not overly expensive but enough to stay out of the cheap category. He looked like the kind of guy who grew up in Oakville and whose parents belonged to a golf club and bought tables at charity fundraisers and ate roast beef dinners on Sunday. Or maybe that thought was from a television show. Though she couldn't remember which one.

One time when they'd made eye contact, his face flushed red when she smiled back, but the elevator door had opened and she'd walked out quickly. She wasn't sure why. Mila had laughed when she told her.

"I see him in the elevator sometimes and I think he's shyer than you. The two of you are going to flash goofy grins for the rest of your lives, wondering if the other one will step it up. Maybe I'll try chatting him up the next time I see him."

"Sure...go ahead and do that. He'll think you're hitting on him." Aria laughed but was nervous at the thought of Mila outing her crush.

"Hmm. You have a point. Well, I don't want to take him away from you. So, I'll just try and find out his dating status. And maybe how much money he makes."

Sometimes, Aria wished Mila lived in the building next door instead of thirteen floors up. Close enough to still hang out. Far enough to stay out of her business.

Aria shoved the last bite of burger into her mouth and chewed, trying not to think about the word 'fat'. She got up and opened the door to her balcony and stepped outside into the cold air. The sweet, earthy smell of cannabis wafted under her nose, combined with sounds of coughing, which meant that the guy from the apartment below was taking his evening break. Across the street, passengers exited from the open doors of the TTC bus and scurried in unison towards the building, like ants racing towards a drop of melted ice cream on a hot sidewalk in summer.

People-watching was a good distraction after a meal, but when the thin woman with the curly red ponytail and muscular calves jogged out the front doors and headed in the direction of the park, Aria felt a wave of nausea hit her stomach and gasped for air. The phantom sour taste of vomit filled her mouth and she felt an urge to run to the bathroom. She grabbed hold of the railing, turned away from the view, closed her eyes, and breathed the way her therapist had taught her. Three short breaths in, count six long breaths out. Repeat. She was swimming…in the ocean…the sun was warm on her face when she turned her head to breathe. Breathe. Salt on her lips. She was back in Cuba, where the bartender turned to watch her emerge from the water. He smiled. The sweetness of coconut water laced with rum replaced the vile taste. She breathed again. And opened her eyes. The elderly man with the plaid jacket was coming out of the front doors; the portly, grey pug cradled in his arms. Another set of breaths and Aria went back inside to pour the last bit of wine into her glass before moving over to the sofa. There wouldn't be anything to watch after the news. She really should cancel the cable. After a few minutes of surfing the channels and stopping to watch a few questions on *Jeopardy*, Aria turned off the TV and picked up her laptop.

It was rush hour on Facebook and she scrolled through the posts, stopping to view photos and avoiding the rants and memes. Mila had recently posted a photo with a new hairdo, pouty lips, and dramatic green eye makeup. Aria clicked thumbs-up. She loved the pic, genuinely. A shot of an eagle in flight appeared next from one of her friends whose wildlife photography skills were improving. Aria gave it a thumbs-up. More scrolling led her to a photo of a couple that made her pause. A woman with dark hair and big eyes was staring into the eyes of a man with a trim beard. Aria wondered which one of her friends had posted this pic. It looked a little too perfect. Professional. She stared. It was hard to tell whether the man was Brown. Half of his face was not visible but the way he held the woman and the adoring look in her eyes indicated they were really into each other. Who was it?

Aria shifted her gaze from the couple and focused on the blue water in the background. That's when she saw the caption. An ad. It made sense since the ethnicity of the couples wasn't clear; they could be South Asian, Italian, Spanish...covering all the bases and appealing to a larger crowd. Usually, she would scroll past such ads but this time the words caught her attention. "Stop looking in all the wrong places. Here's where the quality singles are waiting." She clicked on the photo.

Suddenly she was on another website, with a banner that read LoveinTO - a dating site for people in Toronto. She wanted to look at more pictures but questions started popping up. A username, her birthday, and marital status. No commitment required, it said.

Aria used the same password that she used to sign into her computer at work and suddenly there were headshots of good-looking men who were single and waiting to meet her. But she couldn't read their profiles, which was annoying. Another box revealed a promotion. A six-month subscription for half price. $9.99 per month instead of $19.99. $60. She thought about it for a moment. It was the price of a new pair of shoes on sale, if she was lucky; something she hadn't bought in a long time. She pulled out her wallet and entered her Visa number. In a matter of minutes, she was a member, and right away, a list of matches appeared. Men who lived in her area, were single, and waiting to meet.

Sitting back in her chair, her hand resting on the mouse, the thought hit her. She was now a member of a dating site. How did this happen? Was she ready for this and what if she saw someone that she knew, like Tyler or someone from work?

Aria stared at her picture on the screen. Maybe she hadn't picked the best photo for the profile. She moved the mouse and clicked through a few more of her pics. Maybe this was a mistake. Her hand paused again and then she moved it to the 'account' option. The mouse hovered over 'delete account'. She would lose her money. After a few minutes, she allowed her hand to manoeuvre the mouse and click on the first match. A photo popped up. Ruddy-faced like Prince Harry. She scanned the profile, reading about his love for race cars. Another click.

The pics of the men weren't the same as the ones that had intrigued her to sign up. Lots of selfies with overemphasized noses, which is the effect selfies create unless you tilt your head in a way so the nose isn't too close to the camera. There were photos of guys leaning against their cars, wearing muscle shirts, arms crossed; a man wearing a suit taking a selfie in what looked like a changeroom; another guy posing with his white poodle that was wearing a plaid coat and matching boots. She clicked through more than twenty or so profiles before stopping at one that stood out. Light hair, blue eyes, casual smile. What was so familiar about this one? Aria clicked on the profile and read his introduction. He was forty, divorced, no kids, looking for a woman who liked movies, restaurants and, although he didn't have one, he liked dogs. He called Toronto's west end home and a photo showed him on a bike at the Humber Bay Bridge. There was another photo where he was sitting at a table with a burger in front of him. Aria peered closely at the familiar setting. Those tables...they were the ones on Woody's patio.

It was the light-haired guy from the elevator.

Two

It wasn't an ideal settlement but at least the divorce was final. Her lawyer wasn't more competent than his, but exceptionally determined perhaps. Gutsy. And she had played the gender card, arguing that even though Tanya made more money, she was still entitled to her share of the profits from the condo, and she wasn't expected to pay alimony. What kind of a man would take alimony from his wife anyway, especially when he earned a good living?

Rob had no intention of asking Tanya for money. He just wanted out. She could have the condo and pay him his share. They split the RSPs and the little bit of savings and they were done. Now, he had to pay his legal fees. He suspected that Tanya got off easy since one of her friends from the firm handled her case. Reyah. "A real ball-buster," Tanya would say. Reyah had been over to their place for dinner a couple of times and Rob always suspected she never liked him. She was always throwing icy glances in his direction with those large hazel eyes from her Kashmiri background (according to Tanya). He'd never heard of Kashmir before so, after a subtle eye roll, Tanya explained. "The northern part of the Indian continent." And she went on to explain the history, most of which he'd forgotten since, except the part about the ongoing political strife. It seemed fitting with Reyah's demeanour. She was definitely an attractive woman, and really sharp. He imagined those eyes boring into the souls of her adversaries when arguing her cases. Intimidating. It was easier to let Tanya do all the talking while he sipped wine and that seemed to suit the two women just fine. They never seemed to tire of endless chatter.

The streetcar slowed and Rob stepped onto the street. His building loomed ahead with yellow lights streaming through the square windows as the evening darkened. He had moved into the building just off Roncesvalles Avenue only two years ago. When he and Tanya had parted ways, he'd reluctantly agreed to live with his mom in the Etobicoke house where he had grown up, until he found a place of his own. The house was more than big enough for the two of them to exist without running into one another too often. Besides, his mom spent her winters in Florida with her sister. So, when she'd offered, it made sense. But after a year of sleeping in his old bedroom with Wayne Gretzky watching over him every night and her raised eyebrows as she pretended to read the paper on Sunday mornings when he shuffled towards the coffee pot, he figured it was time find his own place.

"You're going to waste money on rent," his mother kept saying. "Stay here. I'm gone half the time anyway."

So he stayed one more year. His mother never asked questions. She spoke with facial expressions, which he'd learned to read a long time ago. English parents—they hardly opened their mouths to speak. Not like Tanya's family. Portuguese and animated. They yelled at one another all the time. Held nothing back.

"We're not yelling," Tanya would say. "This is how we talk to one another. Your mother goes around with those pinched lips and raised eyebrows like she's horrified at everything!"

She had a point. His mother was nothing like Tanya's mother and aunts. At family gatherings, while everyone was laughing and hugging and telling stories about people that weren't there, his mom stayed quiet, sipping tea by holding the cup handle with the tips of two fingers as if she was sitting with the queen. And she probably believed it could happen someday.

Her family still lived in England in the same working-class area in Yorkshire. Her father had worked in the mines his entire life until they closed, and then he was forced to find labour jobs when he could get them. Her mother had cleaned offices. But she never talked much about her parents. She had shut that door when she moved to Canada. Even when his grandmother died, she'd been reluctant to go back for the funeral.

Rob's father had been working at a London bank all those years ago when he had run into his future wife in the elevator of the building. She was holding a fish-and-chips dinner bundled in newspaper for her mother who was vacuuming the twelfth floor. The college she attended was just around the corner and she would pick up two orders of cod and thick-cut fries and the two would head over to the president's office and sit on his couch, spreading out their meal on his coffee table, being careful not to touch the leather with greasy hands. Afterwards, they were always careful to dispose of the oil-stained newspaper wrapping in the garbage bag that was thrown in the dumpster behind the building before locking the office for the night.

Rob's mother was delicately pretty with blonde hair and crystal eyes. There was talk among her family that aristocratic blood ran through her veins. Perhaps royalty born out of wedlock. It was too bad she grew up in a poor family. There was hope that someday, she would make it out. That opportunity presented itself when she met Rob's father in the elevator that evening while holding her fish and chip dinner.

When they decided to marry, his father didn't even have to ask—she'd already packed her bags for Toronto. Inviting her family to the wedding was an ordeal, but she managed to get through it, sending them back as soon as she could, without being obvious. Her life in England was gone and she didn't want any reminders of the working-class neighbourhood that was part of her upbringing.

Tanya had put herself through law school. Her father worked as an electrician and her mother cleaned houses. She had her own cleaning business, so the money was pretty good. But his mother couldn't accept that he had chosen the maid's daughter for his wife.

"What about Sarah? That lovely girl you dated in high school?"

"I believe she got married."

"To whom? Didn't her father just retire from that bank, I can't remember which one, RBC maybe?"

"I don't know who she married. I'm not in touch with her. Anyway, Mom, your mother was a maid."

"No. She worked as a caretaker in an office building. It is very different. She didn't do other people's dirty dishes."

Rob rolled his eyes but gave a slight nod. "Oh right."

When the Banerjee family moved into the Kingsway neighbourhood just a few doors down from his parents' house, his mother had been concerned. There are no Indian people living in this area, she said. Didn't they want to be around their own kind? Brampton had lovely homes.

Eventually, his mother learned that both Mr. and Mrs. Banerjee were doctors and quickly carried over a bottle of Decoy and a rose bush for their garden. Their son, Ash, came over sometimes when Rob was a kid and they would play video games in the basement and Ash always pulled the pepperoni off his pizza slices. Rob's mother was always friendly to Ash, but she couldn't wrap her head around the fact that the Banerjees didn't eat beef.

"What's wrong with beef tenderloin?" she argued when she was making plans to invite the family over for dinner one Sunday.

"Didn't I mention the Banerjees are Hindu? They don't eat beef." Rob figured she knew given the pepperoni situation.

"What do you mean they don't eat beef? Who doesn't?"

"They don't. It's against their religion."

"What kind of a religion forces you to do something like that?"

"Well, it appears that Hinduism is such a religion. Cows are considered part of the family back in India. Like pets I believe, and they're considered sacred." Rob remembered reading this or hearing this somewhere but he wasn't certain.

"Like pets?"

"Yeah. It would be the same if we ate dogs."

"That's ridiculous!" She was being overly dramatic. "Why would we eat dogs? So, what does that mean? They worship cows? Tenderloin is a very high-priced piece of cow."

Rob rolled his eyes and managed to convince her that lamb was far more extravagant, so she ordered a rack from the butcher.

He had stopped challenging her ignorance years earlier when he couldn't decide if she was blinded by unconscious bias or simply wanted to reaffirm her own status by finding faults in other cultures. Either way, her behaviour embarrassed him.

His mother was polite to Tanya but her pursed lips when they announced their engagement was enough to let him know she didn't approve. The wedding was another story. "What is wrong with a catered brunch at the golf club?" she asked. She would pay for the whole thing. But Tanya wanted a party and her family wanted an open bar. He didn't spend time worrying about his mother's raised eyebrows at his wedding, even when Tanya brought it up a few times. But in her true fashion, his mother stored the memory and resurrected it when he announced the separation.

"Well, I knew at the wedding that she was not the right girl for you. Too flamboyant really."

Tanya's hair was a mass of curls—'unruly' according to his mother—and her skin didn't have the pink undertone of a typical Caucasian woman. 'Olive' his mother used to say.

But now it was over and he didn't have to hear about it anymore.

Rob entered the lobby of the building and as he reached over to push the button to go up to his apartment, he remembered the dirty clothes in his gym bag, inside the trunk of his car in the garage. So he pushed the down button instead.

When he got to P1, a crowd was waiting to go up and he wedged through them to get through the glass doors and out to his car. He rifled in his gym bag and pulled out the shirt, holding it close to his nose. It didn't smell that bad, but maybe he should wash it anyway. He didn't inspect the shorts or the socks, and decided to take the whole bag upstairs instead of walking around with dirty laundry in his hands. Slamming the trunk door shut, he headed back to the lobby. The owner of the condo didn't have a parking spot, so he had to rent one from someone else. It was at the far end of the garage but at least it was on P1 and he didn't have to circle down the ramps to get to the deep underground.

Rob opened the glass door of the garage and stepped into the lobby. The crowd was gone and the only person waiting for the elevator was that pretty woman with the big eyes who parked close to the garage entrance. She glanced at him sideways and then looked away.

He remembered seeing her around a few times since he'd moved into the building. She was usually in the pool when he walked by on his way to the gym on the third floor. He recalled the last time he had seen her—head above the water, hair slicked back, water droplets on her lips. He remembered slowing his pace once to watch as she thrust her arms in front of her, head down, and pushed away from the side of the pool with her feet; her body slicing through the water. She was a strong swimmer. Once, after reaching the other side of the pool, she stopped and glanced in his direction. The action made him step back and he walked the other way, wondering if she had noticed that he'd been watching. He had wanted to see her get out of the pool. From what he could see, it seemed like she was wearing a bikini.

Several times afterwards, he ran into her in the elevator. Mostly, it was during weekday mornings. Sometimes she wore a skirt and he'd peeked at her legs once when he was exiting the elevator on the ground floor to catch the streetcar. She always pushed P1.

Afterwards, he wondered why he didn't introduce himself. She always seemed focused on the elevator buttons and he wasn't sure what to say.

"Good morning, my name is Rob, what's yours?" It seemed awkward somehow.

A couple of times he saw her with a taller woman—Filipino looking, he thought, like his friend's wife. He remembered the woman looking right at him and saying hello. He responded but it seemed so fast and they were in and out of the elevator in no time.

Now, as he stood beside her while they waited for the elevator, he considered making small talk. “This elevator certainly takes its time, doesn’t it,” or maybe “It looks like the top button is broken. It’s pointing downward.” But as he prepared to say the words, the light went off and the doors slid open. The woman who parked beside him came out, pushing her baby in the stroller. He let her walk by and waited for the woman with the big eyes to enter before stepping in. They were alone and she was carrying a bag that smelled like something grilled. Burgers. When was the last time he had gone to Woody’s?

Three

"The same guys are on every site," Naomi said before popping a piece of the Dragon roll into her mouth and grabbing it with her teeth so as not to smear her lipstick.

"Maybe." Aria had finished half of the fish taco and wiped her lip with the napkin to remove a smear of guacamole. "But it's the virtual club scene where you can be at all the clubs at the same time. How else can you do that?"

"Dunno. I'll ask Mike if he knows anyone from work. Lots of cute, single guys at the bank."

"A banker. How fun."

"Finance guys make lots of money, Aria, and that's the only reason they're there. The money comes in handy when they want to buy cottages and take their girlfriends on trips." Naomi popped the last piece of maki into her mouth and gave Aria a sideways glance.

Tyler was a teacher. He wore plaid shirts and jeans and went to his friends' cottages, knowing that he may never have his own, and that was okay with him.

"Why is money such a top requirement?" Aria sipped her Pinot Grigio, holding the liquid in her mouth for a few seconds before swallowing. The taste lingered on her tongue and left an acidic aftertaste. What did she expect from a Happy Hour special?

"Why is it not? That's your problem. You always go for guys who are broke. It's just as easy to fall for a guy who has money than one who doesn't." Naomi gestured to the bartender for another martini. Aria wanted to protest; not the martini but the statement, even though she knew it was true. She found herself dating men who didn't have much money or didn't want to spend it even if they did. She never expected them to pay for dates, even when Naomi kept insisting that men respected women that didn't pull out their wallets when the cheque came. Women should demand to be treated and men should want to feel needed.

Maybe if she'd grown up rich like Naomi, money would be more important to her. Maybe she just didn't fully appreciate the thrill of staying in five-star hotels or owning several Coach handbags that were bought at full price just because she wanted a variety of colours.

Mike had bought handbags for Naomi when they had begun dating five years earlier. Naomi recounted the story nonchalantly, as if he'd paid for two scoops of ice cream. She had guided him into the store at Sherway Gardens, wandered around until she found the bag etched with the famous brown Cs and red leather accents, and said she wanted it. That was that. He took it to the counter, pulled out his Gold Visa, and handed Naomi the paper bag. It was their third date.

The couple met when he was in town with his family from Jamaica for a $500 per plate charity fundraiser for the Herbie Fund—the charity that provided medical treatment to children from the Caribbean. "Old money," Naomi always said when describing Mike's family. His grandparents owned hotels back home and Mike grew up with servants who ironed his shirts and a chauffeur who drove him to private school.

Naomi's father was the surgeon who had operated on Mike's cousin who'd come over from Jamaica years earlier, thanks to his parents' generosity. Naomi and Mike found themselves sitting beside one another at the dinner table, elbows barely grazing as they neatly cut into their salmon wellingtons.

Naturally, it was a setup, Naomi had insisted. It was the first time she had approved of her parents' meddling, but she never said so. She let on as if she didn't notice anything interesting about him at first, but eventually he grew on her—after much effort on his part. Aria knew the truth though. Mike held Naomi's heart the moment he extended his hand to say hello.

Naomi lifted the martini glass to her mouth, her two-carat diamond ring catching the light in a starburst glare. Mike had proposed last year, and the ring dominated Naomi's tiny hands, but Aria couldn't imagine anything smaller for her best friend.

"So hey…I saw that guy from the elevator on the dating site." Aria had held off long enough. She needed to talk about it.

"Which guy?"

"You know, the light-haired one that blushes but hardly says hello."

"Light-haired? Like blonde? I don't remember." Naomi pulled the olive from the toothpick with her teeth and licked her lips. How was it possible that she'd inherited the best features from each of her parents' racial backgrounds, Mila had said to Aria once. Almond-shaped eyes and silky hair from her mother's Chinese heritage, toffee skin and full lips from her father's African roots. Both of her parents were born on the same Caribbean island but met when they came to Canada in the late 70s, drawn together by their shared heritage.

"Well, I told you about him a few times." Aria tried to keep the annoyance out of her voice. Of course, Naomi wouldn't remember. He was just a guy that she had run into in the elevator a handful of times. They had barely said two words to one another. He was a stranger. Insignificant.

"Another white guy?" Naomi never minced her words.

"Yes," Aria answered without looking up, knowing where the conversation was going.

"You know Ari, I get it. You meet a lot of white guys and there's nothing wrong with dating someone from another race. I mean, look at Mike. He's Black from both parents, and my father is Black. But we're both from Jamaica and there's a cultural understanding."

Aria knew where she was going.

"Tyler's family could not understand your background! I mean honestly. His mother assumed that you were Black because you're from the Caribbean. Who doesn't know that Indians also live there? I mean, they're half the friggin' population!"

When Tyler first introduced Aria to his parents, his mother had asked about her hair.

"Do you straighten it, dear?"

"Oh no, this is natural."

His mother looked confused and said nothing for a moment. Then she commented in her blunt manner. "I didn't think Black people had straight hair."

"Oh, I'm not Black," Aria responded.

Tyler's mom looked at her son and then back at Aria. "But I thought Tyler said you are from the Caribbean?"

"Yes, Trinidad actually. That's where my family is from. I was born here."

"Oh, so being born here would make your hair straighter?" Aria had tried not to laugh but she was certain her mouth dropped open as she stared into the confused woman's wide green eyes and realized she wasn't joking.

That's when Aria realized it was time for the history lesson. "The Caribbean is a multicultural group of islands," she explained, immediately going into educator mode as though she was standing in a classroom filled with wide-eyed kids. "The island is made up of almost forty percent people from Indian heritage, forty from African heritage, and the rest are of Chinese heritage, and European and the original Indigenous people." She had recited the statement so many times that it came out like a script.

"Oh, I see. How did that happen?" The forehead was still wrinkled in uncertainty.

Aria didn't want to sound annoyed. How did someone live in Canada her entire life and not know this? Especially in Toronto, with so many Caribbean grocery stores and restaurants. Plus, unlike many other cultures, people from the islands didn't flock together in one community. They lived all over the city among other cultures. That's the way it is back home in Trinidad, her father always said. He often shook his head at the neatly segregated cultural communities across the city: little India, little Italy, Chinatown, Greektown. Why bother coming here? he used to say. Although she never openly agreed with him, Aria asked herself similar questions.

Sometimes he would reminisce about Diwali, the Hindu holiday that was branded 'Festival of Lights' so Westerners could better understand the story of Rama, the triumph of light over darkness and the invitation to Lakshmi into one's home. When Aria was growing up, it was a day when the family refrained from eating meat, lit clay lamps at sundown, and said prayers before eating. And according to her father, in Trinidad dinner guests were usually neighbours and friends who were Christians or Muslims. The whole idea was to share the food, the culture, and the holiday with others.

Aria wondered if she should get into those details with Tyler's mother, who looked skeptical as the lesson was relayed. But she figured that would be confusing since Diwali was a tradition from the Indian ancestors and maybe it would be too much info for his mother, who still couldn't seem to grasp the 'not-Black-but-Brown' concept.

She decided to keep it high level for the first time.

"Oh, the Indians and Chinese went to the islands back in the early 1800s I think...they went as labourers and to start a new life. The Africans were brought as enslaved peoples in the 1600s. I believe it was the Dutch who brought them over. I can't remember." Tyler's mother's eyes widened at the word 'Dutch'.

"Anyway, once slavery was abolished, people had already built lives and they came together to form one culture. So, the food is an amalgamation of the various cultures."

"So, your family is from India? Okay I see. So, you must speak Hindu."

Aria stifled a laugh and remained composed. "No, I don't speak Hindi. The language was lost a bit when the cultures came together. Everyone speaks English with phrases from the other cultures such as Spanish, Hindi, French, et cetera.

"But my parents are Hindu, which is a religion." After saying it, Aria realized it was too much information too soon, because Tyler's mom looked even more confused. But she continued to ask.

"So you eat a lot of curried foods?"

"Yes, but it's a different style of curry than what is eaten in the South Asian countries," and as she watched Tyler's mother's eyes narrow in suspicion, she added, "countries like India, et cetera." She had spoken too fast and the feeling of defensiveness had crept up on her. Aria wanted the conversation to stop but was in too deep by that point.

"Oh, I see." Tyler's mother's eyebrow was raised at that point.

Aria continued to explain that the food was made up of Indian, African, Chinese, French, Spanish, and British fare—all amalgamated to create a unique Caribbean cuisine. Tyler's mom seemed fascinated and asked for details of how the food was prepared. It wasn't a bad conversation in the end because it took up a couple of hours and then it was time to go home. But Aria wasn't convinced that his mother really understood the lesson.

Later, Tyler told her he'd learned something too. Aria thought it was odd that he wouldn't understand Caribbean culture, living in Toronto and going to a multicultural school in Scarborough, but she shrugged it off. It wasn't a bad thing that they both learned something new. Maybe they would pass it along.

Naomi wasn't as open-minded.

"Okay, maybe you taught them something they should have already known, but it says to me that they are just living in their own little box and don't really want to understand other cultures. It's too much work. So, they will always think you are either Black or South Asian and try to lump you into one or the other. People like that never really understand because they don't care to."

Naomi often brought up the same conversation when Aria was dating Tyler. He was 'too white' and would never really commit to her, and why couldn't Aria find a guy from the Caribbean, like Mike?

This time, she spared Aria the lecture and focused on the wealth aspect.

"Maybe Mike knows someone who works at the hospital. A doctor would be nice, right?" Naomi put her hand on Aria's and smiled. Despite the tough-girl posturing, she always had good intentions.

When Aria walked back to the subway, her headache had worsened from the cheap wine and she regretted not letting Naomi buy her a drink. But, somehow, it never felt even when she did.

The subway car was relatively empty, with only a few sleepy-eyed people in crinkly suits. A man's head bobbed loosely on his slumped body and Aria wondered if the movement of the train would catapult him forward onto the dirty floor. As if reading her thoughts, the man jerked upward, eyes wide, trying to make out his whereabouts. She averted her eyes so he wouldn't feel embarrassed.

Aria stood up as the train began to slow down and 'Dundas West' flashed by. A slight breeze accompanied her on the three-block walk to the building and she inhaled the cool air, wondering how Bath and Body Works got the formula for their 'Leaves' candles. There was no perfumed scent in the air of wet, rotting leaves under her feet, or of the aging ones clinging weakly on the trees. But it was a smell she liked from her second favourite season. Autumn was usually everyone's favourite season, with the vibrant colours of death, but for Aria, spring was the promise of a new start, renewed vows, and birth.

She fished out her cell phone and checked the dating app. Coloured icons indicated a few new smiles and one waiting message. Aria touched the envelope icon, her heart hitting her chest. She clicked on the tiny photo that was barely visible. A man with a beard and ponytail taking a selfie in what looked like his bathroom mirror peered at her. Disappointment hit the bottom of her stomach and she closed the app and slid the phone back into her purse.

As she approached the building, the shape of a slightly bent Mrs. DaSilva pulling her dog toward the front doors came into view.

"Angel, come on," the older lady was trying to coax him inside, but he stood firm, a yellow leaf stuck to the matted grey fur on his foot.

"Hi Angel." Aria bent to touch his shaggy head. "What's up buddy?" The dog looked up with his cloudy eyes and wagged his tiny, fuzzy tail.

"He loves this weather because it is not too hot and not too cold."

Mrs. DaSilva lived alone on the first floor. Since Aria had moved into the building, she often saw the older lady walking the dog, pulling her grocery cart down the street from Loblaws, and sitting alone among the crowd at the annual meetings. Aria wondered whether she had family or if she spent Christmases alone with Angel. She considered taking her some cookies during the holidays or offering to walk Angel when the weather was bad, but she never got around to it. Maybe Mrs. DaSilva would see it as charity.

"Come on little one, let's go inside," Aria beckoned the dog, who blinked his round eyes and then turned his head and gazed behind him, feet planted on the ground.

"Okay, a few minutes longer." Mrs. DaSilva turned around to head back onto the street with Angel leading.

A couple of people stood in front of the elevators. A young woman with acrylic nails was scrolling through her phone with one hand, a white plastic bag in the other hand that formed the shape of a rectangle—likely a Styrofoam container from a takeout place. One elevator was still broken. Aria placed herself where she could look in the mirror and passed a hand over her windblown hair. Static cling again.

Finally, the G showed up on the screen above the elevator doors. Aria let the others enter before following. She pushed her floor and, as she stood facing the entrance at the front of the crowd, she saw someone run up to the doors just as they were closing. It was the guy with the braids whom she often saw through the glass walls of the gym when she was on her way to the pool. He was hard to not notice. Sweat dripped down the sides of his determined face as he jogged on the treadmill. It was admirable. But when she got a quick glance at the McDonald's paper bag in his hand just as the doors shut in his annoyed face, she frowned, wondering how he would ever lose the weight if he kept eating junk food.

Once inside the apartment, Aria threw her coat on the stool by the entrance and went to her laptop. Blond elevator-guy's profile was saved in her 'Favourites' section and she looked for the bright blue star that indicated if he was online. He wasn't.

She read his profile again.

> *I'm a professional man living in Toronto, looking to meet an active lady who shares similar interests. I like the outdoors, trying new restaurants, and travelling. Wine, good food, coffee, and sailing are essentials in my life and although I don't have a pet, I would be happy to meet your dog.*

It was well-written. Straight to the point and nothing about wanting to meet his soulmate. No spelling or grammar mistakes either, and he liked dogs. She liked all the same things that he had listed, except sailing, because the last time Naomi and Mike took her on a sailboat, she threw up.

"Seasick," Naomi had said, handing her a cloth to wipe under her chin, as she bent over the toilet. "No other reason, right?" Aria took the cloth and looked at her friend's face. What other reason could there be?

What would she tell him if he asked her to go sailing? Aria closed the page. She hadn't read his preferences and couldn't bear to see that he was looking for a twenty-five-year-old blonde athlete who loved to sail. Maybe he wanted to continue the wasp bloodline and move to the Kingsway where their kids would attend private school and spend winter vacations in private ski resorts and summers at the yacht club.

Tyler's new girlfriend was blonde. When Aria had run into them last summer at Cactus Club, she was on her way to the washroom. Naomi was following close behind. When Tyler called her name, she wasn't prepared to see him sitting across from the petite blonde with an overbite. Aria had moved closer to the table where they sat; the blonde girl's face flushed a bit as she shook Aria's hand. Tyler made small talk, something about his first time trying Cactus Club since it had opened and that they had wanted to try it based on all the great reviews about the place. He was babbling and Aria nodded, saying a few polite words before feeling Naomi's hand on the small of her back, indicating it was time to say goodbye and continue to the washroom.

"That won't last," Naomi said when the door to the washroom closed behind them.

"No? Why do you say that?"

"Well, come on. She said two words and I'm surprised she was able to put those words together in the first place. And what a massive overbite. I bet he doesn't stop reminding her about it."

"I dunno…she's kind of pretty." Aria wasn't sure why she said that and then added, "I guess."

"Sure, bleached blonde and white wonder bread. Tyler is so insecure that he can't date someone who looks better than him but I knew he would choose someone like that. So in that case, I change my verdict. Maybe it will last because he feels better about himself every time he sees those buck teeth. Plus she is skinny…wow!" At the last words, Naomi glanced over at Aria, regret in her eyes, and quickly changed the topic.

"His mother is probably relieved that he is not dating a 'Black' girl who can't admit she's Black…" Naomi giggled at the memory. After the history lesson with Tyler's mother, he told Aria that his mother wanted to know if she was ashamed of being Black because she really didn't believe that Brown people came from the Caribbean.

Aria had not responded to Naomi's comment, but once she was sitting on the toilet inside the stall, she let herself laugh out loud and felt the relief as Tyler and the urine exited her body.

These memories gave her a little boost and she logged back into the website and clicked on the light-haired guy's profile, scrolling down to his preferences.

He was looking for a woman who was between thirty to forty, who was spiritual but not religious, like himself. She should be between 5'2 and 5'7 because he was 5'10. He didn't care if she had been married before, because he was divorced with no kids. Finally, she scrolled down to read his preferred ethnicities: No preference.

Aria clicked on the smiley face and a message popped up. "Thank you. You smiled at this member." And she closed her computer.

Four

Rob checked his phone. She should be arriving soon. The only time she'd ever showed up late was on their first date.

He'd arrived at the restaurant early, so he could order a draft before she graced him with her presence. There was going to be drama. She was just a few weeks shy of asking him to plan the wedding.

As far as he was concerned, it wasn't a relationship. Sure, they were seeing each other a couple of times a week and he wasn't dating anyone else. But he just didn't have time, and now as he sat and waited to break up with her, he realized that maybe he just wasn't ready.

The divorce with Tanya was simple, because they didn't disagree on terms. It had been more tiring and more painful than he'd expected. Although at the time, he didn't realize he was in pain.

He wanted to leave the marriage, so he figured it would just be a relief. And initially it really was. But one day, his director at work called him in for a meeting. Apparently, there was talk around the office about his mood. He had snapped at a few people in meetings, and someone actually complained to HR that he was yelling at his staff. Rob was confused. He didn't recall any of these incidents in the way they were described. Sure, he had to be stern a couple of times when someone in a meeting didn't listen or when staff weren't meeting deadlines. But it was all work related. He'd needed to get the job done and sometimes it meant being a bit more forceful.

His director listened to his rationale, and while she didn't disagree, she came right out and asked if he was dealing with a personal issue. Rob didn't know how to respond. It wasn't any of her business, but the way she looked at him in silence meant she knew the answer.

Without any more questions, she handed him the card of the HR consultant in the office and said that the benefits plan provided coverage to get some support. She never used the word 'therapist,' like his mother did.

Rob was reluctant and embarrassed, but he followed through and made an appointment.

At first, he was rolling his eyes, wondering how this man sitting across from him could help at all. The guy seemed quite young and crossed his legs a lot. But he went back the second time, and then the third, and realized he was in pain. He wanted the divorce but, somehow, he felt he had failed Tanya.

She was a vibrant, headstrong lawyer—the many reasons he had fallen for her. Tanya was different from his mother. She didn't care about the perfect house in the affluent neighbourhood. She liked the Toronto condo life and, despite her salary, she was always looking for a sale. She wanted kids, she was a great cook, and didn't worry too much about calories.

Tanya was smarter than he was and quicker and sharper. Therapy made him admit that he just couldn't keep up.

Maybe he wasn't ready for everything she wanted after all. But when the therapist tried to get him to admit that he felt inadequate, Rob decided he'd had enough sessions. He knew he needed time to mourn the loss.

Rob decided to be mindful of the way he spoke to staff and in meetings. And as far as he was concerned, that was all he needed to do—some posturing for work. He didn't need to figure it all out right then.

When he signed the divorce papers, his mother urged him to get out and start dating.

"Don't worry darling, she just wasn't the right girl. Far too pushy really. You need to find someone who is less of a whirlwind and more settled." And then she had added, "Besides, she was starting to put on a bit of weight. I mean it wasn't a lot really, but those women tend to start getting hippy right after marriage as if they don't feel the need to try anymore. There are many women out there who maintain trim figures throughout their relationships."

He ignored the comment because it wasn't worth the discussion. She would just act all innocent, as if she didn't realize she was being rude.

But dating was not on Rob's mind. He couldn't imagine the thought of sex with anyone else. For the first time in his life, it seemed scary. He couldn't imagine taking off his clothes in front of a stranger who would see his soft belly—the result of Tanya's cooking and the many pub dinners after they broke up.

So he joined a gym and most of his evenings were spent on the rowing machine or pumping iron. He busied himself working overtime and, to the delight of his boss, kept his head down in the coffee room and on the way to the washroom when rumours of his single status hit the gossip lines in the office. He ate lunch at his desk or went for a walk down the street and grabbed something a couple of blocks away from his office so he wouldn't run into one of the handful of women who brushed his arm accidentally when he washed his mug in the sink. He was forced to flick his eyes to theirs when giggled apologies cut the silence in the air. "No worries," he would mumble as he scooted back to the confines of his cubicle.

A couple of years later, when he was having Friday night drinks with the guys, the topic of dating apps came up.

"Some of the women are just looking for sex," one of his buddies said. "No strings."

Rob couldn't imagine there were women who could just have sex and walk away. If he'd learned one thing from his marriage, it was that women's libidos are tied to their minds. Tanya was a headstrong woman, but if she was upset, sex wasn't an option. She wanted to be held, cuddled. In bed, she was soft and tender, nothing like the vicious wolf who safeguarded her clients.

He supposed it was possible there were women closer to the male end of the spectrum. He didn't have too much experience with those women, since Tanya was only his third girlfriend and the one in high school didn't really count. They'd only get together to make out after school and at school dances. Once or twice, they went to a movie but after graduation, they went to separate schools and he'd heard she got married to someone she met at university.

When he got home that night after drinks, Rob checked out the dating app LoveinTO. His friends had pestered him for most of the evening, saying it was time for him to have sex with a live person and give his hand a break. But he never let on that he was going to try it. He didn't want to answer any questions.

The app was pretty straightforward but he had to commit to a six-month subscription. It was only $10 per month. Less than the price of a craft beer. So he pulled out his Visa and signed up. It took a while before he found a photo of himself that was half decent—one taken at a work conference a few years back.

The application however, was troublesome. Too many questions about preferences. What food did he like; did he prefer dogs, cats, or birds; what was his perfect date night. Rob didn't know how to answer any of the questions, and thankfully, he didn't have to. He did the best he could and left most of it blank. The easy stuff was his age, his personal description, and the checkboxes of what kind of woman he was looking to meet. He left the introduction blank until he could find the words to craft something suitable.

Once he was signed up, the matches were delivered. They didn't look like the ones in the ads, so he had to scroll through the photos until he found one or two that he found attractive. After the first couple of dates, Rob found himself uninterested. The women were nice enough but his mind would wander during conversations over coffee. He just didn't want to be there.

Eventually, his attention lapsed and he was only checking his matches weekly. He was on the app for about two months before he found Emily or, rather, she found him. He saw Emily's message a few days after she had sent it; that's what she told him afterwards.

Emily's profile pulled him in with photos that showed her standing on a mountain in full ski gear, hiking in the summer, and travelling. She'd never been married but had been involved in two long-term relationships. Her photos were alluring. Silky, blonde hair blowing in the wind as she held onto the mast of a sailboat, a shot of her wearing a cocktail dress that showed an athletic figure with perky cleavage that looked natural. Rob usually wasn't attracted to blondes. They reminded him of his mother. But she had a small space between her two front teeth, and thin lips; not a flawless veneer like his mom.

They met before talking on the phone. He usually preferred to hear the voice first but her texts were clever and funny and he found himself checking his phone through the day to see if she had written. She didn't respond to his texts right away. And when he asked if she had met anyone else, she didn't respond. It drove him crazy. Days would go by and nothing. When he had begun chatting with other women on the site, she messaged him again.

She had been busy. But she never answered the question about other men.

So he asked her out for drinks. She accepted after a day passed, giving him two evenings when she was available. Her schedule was hectic because she was an interior designer for a large firm and was working on a project.

Rob had to blow off after-work drinks with his buddies to meet up with her. But it was a monthly ritual to catch up over dinner and beer and it wasn't as if he was missing much.

He made reservations for a table at the restaurant in Yorkville and Emily was going to meet him after work. Usually, he didn't buy dinner on the first date, but he had a feeling she would expect dinner.

She arrived fifteen minutes late. He remembered how she had walked in with an air of nonchalance, her phone held up to her ear. She made her way to the table where he sat and threw him an acknowledging glance as she continued to listen to the person on the other end.

"Rob? Sorry about that. Work is crazy lately. I'm Emily. It's so lovely to finally meet you." Her smile revealed the lovely gap in her teeth.

She looked exactly like her photos. He ordered a bottle of wine and didn't flinch when she ordered the Black Cod.

They slept together on the third date. He'd wanted to take her home the first night but didn't even try. He believed that unwritten taboo that sex on the first date would lead to a quick ending. By the second date, which they scheduled two weeks later due to her 'busy schedule', he was masturbating every time they had a phone conversation. On the third date, he invited her to his place for dinner. She accepted but made him wait another week.

He made chicken vindaloo, because she told him of her fondness for Indian food. The bottled vindaloo sauce made the preparation easy and she seemed to savour every tiny bite in between sips of water. By the time dinner was over, and the bottle of wine was empty, he couldn't wait any longer. The dishes were left in the sink as they made their way to the bedroom, clothes shedding at every step.

It wasn't the way he'd imagined it, though. Once they got into bed, she became passive, lying on her back as her head rolled to one side. It was as if she just wanted to get it over with. He couldn't really hold himself back at that point, so within ten minutes they were lying side by side, shoulders touching.

Maybe it was the wine, he thought.

But the sex wasn't better the second time, or the third. Soon, he found himself having sex with her just to relieve himself. She never initiated either.

After a few weeks, she began asking him about his weekend plans. What was he doing that they couldn't see each other all weekend? He wasn't always busy but some nights he just wanted to be at home alone, watching Netflix and not worrying about answering her questions.

There were questions about his mother and hints that they should meet her for lunch, and more than one mention of the fact that she grew up just north of the Kingsway neighbourhood where his mom lived. But by that time, he had already realized this was not going to evolve into a committed relationship. She wasn't a bad girl, and despite the bland sex, he enjoyed their dates. Her clever wit and banter was entertaining, but he wasn't ready for another serious relationship. Not with Emily, for certain. Rob just couldn't see the two of them together for the long haul.

His mother would love her though, he often thought. Which is why the two could never meet.

"Hey. Why so glum?" Emily's arrival reminded him where he was. A splash of floral tickled his nose as she leaned in and kissed him on the mouth.

"Emily. . . ." He got up and kissed her on the cheek, feeling the knots in his stomach.

"It was quite the day," she said, sliding into the seat. "You know the deal. Clients think they are designers and know colour. Sometimes we just need to give in though."

"Yes, I know how that works."

"This is a large US company opening their headquarters downtown. I originally suggested slate-blue floors for a hint of colour, but they are insisting on grey."

"I suppose it makes a difference to someone who's in charge." Rob managed to laugh.

Emily ordered a glass of wine and opened the menu.

"What are you going to have?" She didn't look up.

Rob hadn't planned to eat. He just wanted to get it over with and leave. But she had just come from work so he figured he might as well buy her dinner before the talk.

"I was looking at the burger."

"Burgers. You always eat burgers. Not healthy, Rob. What would your mom say?"

The knot in his stomach tightened.

She ordered a shrimp salad and he had the burger, medium rare with fries. He wondered how she could eat salad all the time and not want a slab of meat once in a while.

In true Emily style, she chattered over the meal, talking about work and her girls' night out. Her friend Margaret finally got the engagement ring and they would be planning the wedding together. Teal bridesmaid dresses would not be flattering.

Is it blue or green? The colour was just off. She suggested they go with one style and let each woman choose her own colour. More bold colours like royal blue and deep purple.

Rob chewed his burger and chugged his beer, wondering who she would choose for a date. Emily would have no trouble finding the right guy who wanted the same things that she did. She would make the perfect corporate wife, and have beautiful kids who went to private school.

Once their plates were cleared, he resisted the urge to order another beer and began.

"So Em, I wondered if we could have a talk."

Emily stopped patting her mouth with the napkin and her eyebrows crinkled. She put the napkin down and he could see that her eyes suddenly brightened. She leaned in a bit.

"Yes?"

His stomach flipped and he realized what she was expecting. For a moment, he thought he could put it off until the next day. Maybe do it over the phone? It was a selfish thought. She deserved to hear it in person. Tanya used to say that his immaturity showed when he avoided important discussions. "It's like you think the issue will dissolve if you avoid talking about it," she would say. He knew this time the issue wouldn't go away and he had to deal with it now. He leaned over the table a little and smiled at her.

"It's been really great spending time with you these past few months. We've had some great times."

"We sure have." Her smile was sickening.

"The thing is, I am not sure I can give you what you are looking for. I'm not ready for a relationship right now."

The words flew out too quickly. Hard. Emily moved back, eyes wide in shock.

"What?" The word was hurled out of her mouth, and he sat back, wishing he could do it over. Rob watched her for a moment, and automatically leaned over with the intention of taking her hand, but instead he looked into her eyes—narrow and hurt. He breathed deeply and thought carefully about his next words.

"Em, listen, I think you're a great woman. You're beautiful, and you're so successful and smart. I know you'll go places. But…I'm not the guy for you. I don't believe I can give you what you you're looking for."

"What I'm looking for?" Her tone was demanding; her eyes blazing. "And what is that?"

Rob paused before choosing the next response. "Well, perhaps I am wrong, but I believe you're looking for a long-term relationship. And that's not something I can do right now."

"Not what you can do? You mean have a normal life? The life that everyone strives for? You want to live alone in a rented apartment forever?"

Rob said nothing.

"So what are you saying? You're saying this is over?"

"I'm sorry."

"I don't get this. We've been in a relationship for six months. When did you decide that you no longer wanted a real life?"

"We've been dating for six months. I don't think we ever discussed a relationship." He was suddenly annoyed.

"Oh really? So you've been seeing other women?"

"No, I haven't."

"So then it's been exclusive. It's a relationship. And now you've changed your mind, or you always knew? You were just using me? Did you meet someone else online?"

The questions, fired one at a time, were sharp and direct. He said nothing.

"Well?"

"There's no one else. I just don't want to get into something serious right now."

"Right now? Or with me?"

He knew better than to answer the question. The beer was giving him a headache and he needed fresh air. He pulled out his wallet and gestured to the waitress.

"You're leaving? Without talking about it? You're just going to go with no explanation?"

"I've told you Emily. I'm not ready right now."

"It makes no sense. You've been divorced for over a year, so when will you be ready?"

She posed a valid question. He didn't know what he wanted. But he knew that he didn't want her. He didn't want to be standing under a plastic arch waiting for her arrival in a big wedding dress, with people standing around flashing phoney smiles on their faces. He didn't want to live on the Kingsway again and watch the neighbours frown when a Brown or Black family moved into the area.

The cheque arrived and he pulled out a fifty, a twenty, and a ten. He knew the tip was too much but he didn't wait for change.

"I'm sorry Emily. I know you will find someone who is better for you than I could ever be." He heard his own voice sounding almost rehearsed as he slipped on his jacket, eyes focused on the scratch across the table.

"If you don't know what you want at this age, then I am better off without you."

He stared straight ahead as he walked out.

***

Rob entered the foyer of his building and saw the chubby guy with the Kawhi braids waiting for the elevator, McDonald's bag in hand. The waft of fried fast food hit his nose as the guy glanced at him and nodded.

"Hey," Rob said and looked up to see that the elevator had stopped on the seventeenth floor. What was familiar about that floor? He thought for a moment but couldn't pinpoint the number's significance. The elevator made its way down to the ground and Rob stepped inside with his neighbour.

As soon as he entered his apartment, Rob took off his clothes, brushed his teeth, and climbed into bed. He picked up his phone and logged into the dating app. There were a few smiles waiting for him, so he perused through the profiles. He was no longer a paying member so though he could see who liked him and view their profiles, he couldn't communicate with them unless he renewed his subscription.

After he'd met Emily, he let the subscription expire and just fell into the comfortable two-night-per-week routine. Dinner, movies, drinks, and sex. They never went out during the day and they didn't discuss being exclusive. The recent conversation lingered in his mind. Perhaps he should have had the conversation with her about not being exclusive.

He clicked through the new matches. A woman with glasses and a golden retriever smiled back at him. Beautiful looking dog. She had sent him a message but he couldn't read it. Next, was a pretty blonde woman taking a selfie with pouty lips. He swiped to skip. She looked too much like Emily. A curly-haired brunette with blue eyes in a low-cut shirt showing deep cleavage; a pretty Brown woman with big eyes and straight teeth; a fitness instructor with defined abs; a short-haired doctor...wait. He swiped backwards through the previous profiles. The one with the big eyes...she lived in West Toronto; she was thirty-seven; liked hiking, travelling, swimming. She loved the outdoors. She looked familiar. He scrolled through her photos. Thin, brown skin, natural. Maybe he'd met her the last time he was actively seeking someone. He couldn't remember. There were quite a few first dates that never turned into a second. Rob's eyes were starting to close and the pics became fuzzy. He closed the app, reached over and turned off the lamp, and let his head fall onto the pillow.

Five

The alarm sounded just as the faceless man leaned over for a kiss. Aria's eyes snapped open and she looked around. She was in bed, clutching her pillow to her chest. Groaning, Aria rolled over to swipe out the sound of morning bells. The ringtone was called *Morning Sunrise* and was intended to simulate the sun coming up through soothing acoustic guitar tones. Although the tones didn't seem that soothing to Aria—it was too loud.

The building's heat was just a few days shy of being turned on and she felt a chill on her bare arm. She pulled the covers under her chin and rolled over on her side. It was so tempting to snuggle under the covers for a few more moments. Maybe she could call in sick and spend the day in pyjamas, finishing the novel that had been sitting on the bedside table for the past month. But she had two presentations at schools today and couldn't cancel on the kids. Their beaming faces and eager questions were the main reasons Aria liked her job. She snapped open her eyes and forced herself to fling off the covers, braving the nippy air to the bathroom.

As the warm water cascaded over her body, Aria pinched her stomach. It was a habit that would not die. Tyler used to say that it was a good way to measure if her fitness regime was working. The first time they'd showered together, he stopped kissing her and grabbed a piece of her stomach and squeezed. There was a lot more to squeeze back then and she remembers the disappointment on his face as he looked up at her.

His face changed for that moment and his tone was soft. "It's a starting point. Just do this every day and you'll see the progress," he'd said.

So she made it a point to pinch daily until she could only grab a bit of skin. But she never wanted to shower with him after that and always made the excuse that she liked the time to herself. He never protested, but started pinching her stomach when she got into bed every night.

With her hair washed and body soaped, the memory faded. Aria turned off the water and climbed out of the tub. She wiped the water from her body with the towel, brushed her teeth, and applied mascara to lift her sleepy eyes. Her outfit had been picked the night before and was hanging on the back of the door; another habit she made for herself so she wouldn't spend twenty minutes staring into her closet every morning, wondering why she had nothing to wear. Somehow, the clothes didn't look as appealing in the morning as they did at night.

After pouring a glass of orange juice, Aria sat at the kitchen counter and logged onto her laptop. Her hands fumbled as the mouse hovered over the options. Click. Click. Twelve men had viewed her profile in the past twenty-four hours. She had not been online since sending a smile to the light-haired guy. One by one, she scrolled through the photos of men who had checked her out. As she swiped away the fourth one, the light-haired guy's photo showed up. He had viewed her profile the night before. Her heart beat against her chest as she scrolled down to see his actions. Was there a mutual interest? She searched for the words. The signal. The confirmation that he 'smiled' back and was interested.

Aria moved the mouse down the page and got to the end of the light-haired guy's profile. Then she moved it back up. Maybe she missed it. But when she got back to his photo, looking again for the message that said 'This member smiled back at you,' it was not there. Disappointment flooded through her body like a grey wave. He would have seen her smile by now. Or maybe he was busy. Maybe men didn't check as often as women. Thoughts raced through her mind but she shook them off. It was getting late.

She shut down the website and closed the laptop. Draining the last bit of orange juice from her glass, she placed it in the sink beside a few other dishes from the night before.

Almost as soon as she pushed the button, the bell sounded and the elevator doors opened. Aria stepped inside, stifling a yawn. She needed coffee. The doors closed and she leaned back against the back wall, letting her eyelids rest for a moment. The elevator slid downwards, carrying her. Steady. Swiftly. Then a soft jolt. It stopped and Aria snapped open her eyes with barely enough time to focus and look up at the sign that said 14 before the doors flew open and he walked in.

"Morning." And he pushed the G button.

She let out a breath and stood up straight.

"Good morning." She heard the smallness in her voice. Almost a whisper. Her throat was dry.

The elevator moved downward. 12…11…10…9…8… Aria fixated on the numbers with each breath; 7…6…5…4…3…Through the corners of her eyes she saw that he was staring straight ahead. She should say something. But what?

A sudden stop. Ground floor. The chrome doors slid open and he walked out. Silently, the doors closed again.

***

Why didn't u talk to him, Mila texted. Aria could hear Mila's tone through the text; soft and gentle, with a hint of judgement.

I was caught off guard, couldn't speak.

Just open your mouth and talk girl.

Easy for you to say miss chatty.

What could she have said anyway? Nice shoes? She recalled Converse-type sneakers and wondered where he worked that he could pull off sneakers.

He could have said "goodbye" or "have a nice day".

True dat he's a dick. Forget him.

He didn't smile back.

Maybe he didn't see it yet. You know guys. Not a priority. Or maybe he's just stupid. Don't know what to say. Move on.

Maybe he wasn't stupid. Maybe he was just uncomfortable. If another guy in the building had smiled at her, and she wasn't interested, maybe she'd feel the same—boxed into a small space with someone who is drooling over you. A dog standing inside the kennel, big-eyed, pawing at the bars, begging you to take them home and not understanding why you kept walking, avoiding eye contact. The fear of having to explain. No wonder he bolted out of the elevator.

***

Rob looked down at his sneakers as he walked up Roncensvalles Avenue. The morning was a blur and he had grabbed the first pair of shoes that were in front of the door. Hopefully, his boss wouldn't notice and maybe she wouldn't even bother. Their team was pretty casual, even though their dress code specifically stated no running shoes.

He didn't really care that much anyway. The text from Emily had turned his mood sour as soon as he'd rolled over in bed and checked his phone. Served him right to check text messages first thing in the morning. She had sent it in around 1 a.m. Angry, accusing, hysterical—she probably had a few drinks.

He tried to replay the conversation in his mind as he stood in the shower, hot water beating down on his skin. Much of it was a blur. But he remembered her anger, the venom flying out of her mouth. He couldn't blame her. Who doesn't spit poison when someone breaks up with them? But Emily was a catch for the right guy. It wouldn't be long before she found someone else and got over him.

Rob thought about her question. When would he be ready for a relationship? It was a fair question and he didn't know the answer. Maybe he would end up like some of his divorced friends, who slumped over burgers and beer at the local bars on weeknights and woke up on weekend mornings in the beds of random women they met online.

When he finally realized he'd been standing in the shower for some time, Rob emerged to read 7:35 a.m. on the clock. He was usually on his way up to the subway by this time. He pulled on some clothes, skipped the glass of OJ, and headed out to catch the elevator.

***

Cubicles were like tiny caves that allowed one to hide during the workday, unless one's boss was looking for you. Aria sipped from her cup, touching the hot tea with the tip of her tongue before taking a bigger gulp. As she read through the emails, her mind wandered to the encounter in the elevator that morning. What if she had said something to him? "Nice running shoes." Why couldn't she have been that bold woman and lay it all on the table: "So you like to sail, I wouldn't have guessed." He might have laughed and maybe they would've broken into conversation about the dating app. She could have coyly said, "I sent you a smile to see if you would recognize me." Or maybe, "You didn't smile back…." No. That would've put him on the spot.

"Hey Aria, we're going in the lunchroom." A face peered sideways into her cubicle, interrupting the mental drama going on in Aria's head. Fazia. Her toothy smile changed as they locked eyes and she paused, cocking her head to one side. "You okay?"

"Yeah, fine. Um, I'll be there in a minute. Just in the middle of a thought. You know…"

Fazia smirked. "It's lunchtime and all thinking stops for one hour." And her head disappeared.

There were always two lunch shifts. Noon and 1 p.m. Aria ate with the other Health Promoters in her department in the early shift. A couple of times, when a meeting went over, she had to join the 1 p.m. group—the Researchers. They were a subdued, introverted group who talked a lot about news, facts, and numbers. It was the kind of group Aria needed when she wanted to be around people who didn't expect her to talk, laugh, or engage on the days when she could melt into the room, eat her lunch, and let the buzz of talk surround her. Today was not one of those days. She needed to hear from Julie.

As she entered the lunchroom, Aria could see the red-head bobbing up and down, side to side, gesturing hands in the air, and the wide eyes of the other women at the table. Julie was already into one of her dating stories. Aria pushed her container of leftover rice and chicken into the micro-wave and moved closer to the table, trying to make out the words coming from Julie's rapidly moving mouth. Julie was a serial dater who had mastered all of the dating apps on the market and publicized her adventures at lunchtime.

Aria managed to piece together a few words by the time she made it to the table. Apparently, a guy had made it to date four. Julie's green eyes sparkled as she talked, describing each date in detail, from the jeans that hugged his ass ever so tightly to the dribble of beer on his chin that she'd licked off on the third date.

Aria found Fazia at the end of the table and squeezed in beside her. Fazia and Carmen were leaning in as Julie described the actions that took place after the licking of the chin.

The showy redhead was not what people would classify as beautiful woman. Aria found her attractive in a tube kind of way. A tube of mascara, a tube of lipstick, a tube of foundation thickly spread over skin that no one ever saw in the raw. She had great hair though. Short, straight, and thick, stylishly tucked behind the ears with sideburn wisps hanging down the sides of her cheeks, framing her angular face.

Aria found her intimidating. She was loud and wore bright colours as if to scream, "Look at me, listen to me," and her eyes sparkled when people called out her name and asked about the latest man in her life. Or, like that one time, when she'd dated a woman. Aria had never seen the lunchroom so packed. Men from all departments crowded at the table. People started arriving before noon to get a seat closest to the end of the table where the redhead sat, so they could listen to the nuanced details of the blonde workout trainer that was Julie's latest fling.

"Maybe I was always a lesbian. Maybe I just couldn't come out before."

She never crossed the line of inappropriateness. No sexual details were ever pitched out into the air but subtle comments created pictures in the minds of the staff. Even Aria found herself curious. What would it be like to date a woman?

But the affair was over within a few months and seats became available in the lunchroom once again.

Today's talk was more of the same. Aria waited for details about the dating app, but the couple were already in the bedroom by the middle of the lunch hour.

"This sounds a lot like the last one," Carmen said under her breath. The three chuckled.

"Hey, what about you?" Fazia turned to Aria.

"What about me?"

"Any new guys on the horizon?"

"There's a horizon?"

"Yeah, I guess that answers the question."

"Maybe she doesn't want to date just yet." Carmen dismissed Fazia's chiding. "Dating is overrated anyway."

"Well then how did you find your husband?" Fazia turned her questions to Carmen.

"We never dated. We just got married." Carmen gave a sideways grin and the three women laughed.

"So I hear there's a new manager in Health Promotion who got the job over Sangeeta. I think his name is Jack and he looks pretty young."

Aria breathed a silent sigh of relief as the conversation shifted to office gossip. She wasn't ready to talk about the light-haired guy. There was nothing to talk about anyway. He was just the guy in the elevator who she'd happened to match with on a dating app. Was it a coincidence or fate? She wanted to ask the question out loud, but she knew where that would go—opinions turning into unsolicited advice and then a trapped feeling inside, like she had to follow through and provide weekly updates.

As much as she cherished the work friendships, she knew better than to get into her dating situation with the girls.

She had stopped talking about her personal life after she broke up with Tyler. He used to go with her to the company Christmas parties and the summer picnics and people often crossed the floor to say hello. A few times, they had gone to Carmen's house for a barbeque and eaten small portions of meat and green salad, skipping the bread and dessert. Tyler got along really well with Carmen's husband and there was always talk of them going out for evening dates together and maybe even a trip down south. The latter horrified Aria. How would they explain that restaurants were not on their list of places to go? Tyler would insist on a BnB with a kitchen so they could make all of their meals. The idea gave Aria anxiety every time Carmen brought it up.

When they broke up, she didn't go to any of the events for a year, faking conflicting events or illness. People liked Tyler. She wasn't sure they would understand why she let him go. And she never confided in Carmen about the breakup.

Six

Mila opened the door in her pink kimono robe. It was a Christmas gift to herself that one year she'd gotten into an argument with her mother and boycotted the whole family event. After a bottle of wine, she had logged into her Amazon Prime account and picked it from her favorites list. The robe was pure silk and cost around the price of the two other polyester bathrobes from Victoria's Secret she used every day. The silk one was reserved for evenings when she entertained. Aria smiled when she saw the pink silk and felt a little flattered.

"Come on in and let's drink to stupid men!" Mila took the bottle of wine and sashayed into the kitchen.

"What did you make? It smells great!" Aria asked as she took a whiff of the scent.

Mila had recently taken up cooking and was often inviting Aria to taste her meals in return for honest feedback.

"Jerk chicken quesadillas."

"Jamaican and Mexican. Interesting." Aria wasn't surprised.

Mila had been taking it up a notch each time she perfected a meal. She was now in the fusion stage.

"Quesadillas made with chicken that's been jerked. But not the fun way."

Mila poured two glasses of red and they flopped down on her new paisley couch, a purchase for herself after the Valentine's Day when her boyfriend at the time showed up at her place with a box of chocolates from the dollar store.

When Aria moved into the building, she had been driving around the parking garage in search of her assigned space. No one had given her instructions on how to find the space in the underground maze and she was starting to panic. Mila was strolling through the garage when Aria's attention was taken up with the numbers painted on the concrete posts. When she realized there was a person walking in front of her, she hit the brakes, and blinked to see a Filipina in skinny jeans and a pink button-down blouse glaring at her.

"Why don't you watch where you're driving?" Mila yelled, hands on hips, eyes as fiery as the dyed hair with long fringe that touched the top of her eyelids.

"Oh crap, I'm sorry. I've been driving forever and can't find my parking spot. This place is so confusing! Where are the signs anyway?"

The tone of her helpless voice must have been what softened Mila's attitude. With one eye roll and pursed mouth, she walked over to the driver's side and peered into the open window.

"What's the number of your spot?"

"P23."

"Oh, close to the elevator. You must be new and rich to have the close parking spot."

"It came with the unit."

"Well, you must be rich to have that unit. I think you're looking for the one over there. And she pointed her long, pink nail in the direction of Aria's spot.

"Oh, right there. I must be blind. Listen, thank you so much. And I'm sorry I almost hit you. Nice top by the way."

Mila's eyes narrowed and she grinned widely, toothy. "You're welcome. And thanks. I like this shirt too. Calvin Klein." And then she cocked her head slightly before half whispering the last word, "Winners."

"Oh, I love Winners! I'm Aria by the way, and I just moved into 1702."

"Mila. 2704. Nice to meet you, Aria. Keep your eyes on the road when you're driving."

"I will. Thanks again."

They ran into each other again that evening in the elevator when Aria was taking down some recycling.

"See that's what happens. You move all of your shit because you can't decide what to bring and then you end up throwing it away. Paid for movers and all?" Mila was wearing light blue flannel pj's with a martini-glass print.

"Um, yeah, I had a couple of movers. I mean, it's easier than asking friends."

"True dat. You don't have to spend money on pizza and beer and have your friends break all of your stuff. Hire professionals to do what they do best."

"Yeah, movers is the only option really. They get the job done."

Only then did Aria realize Mila was transgender. The tall woman was standing close, facing her with inquisitive eyes and Aria noticed the bump in her throat that seemed unusual. At first, she wasn't sure why it would be unusual. She must have been staring because the tall woman narrowed her eyes and gave her a look. Aria turned away just as the revelation came to mind—only men had Adam's apples.

They kept running into each other after that encounter as if they both kept magnets in their pockets and couldn't help but steer towards the other. At first Aria wasn't sure how to address Mila. She worried that she wouldn't use the right pronouns. Did the woman prefer she or they? It was not a question you could just blurt out. But after several encounters, she began to relax and stopped thinking about the pronouns. Given her easygoing manner, she figured Mila would just correct her if there was a mistake by saying something sarcastic and then laughing it off.

The encounters became so frequent that Mila joked about being stalked. "If you want my number, just ask!" At that point they did exchange numbers and Mila invited Aria to her place for dinner.

The first time she sat down at Mila's table, a plate was set in front of her with garlicky-smelling fried rice and two chicken legs. Adobo, Mila said. Filipino food. She was just starting out with her mother's recipes.

Mila had watched as Aria took a bite. A small bite.

"What? You don't like it?" Mila's eyes were wide. "What's wrong? Too much garlic?"

"No, it's delicious. I just…I mean, I don't eat a lot…big meals I mean. I just take small bites." Aria didn't know what to say. She was still in therapy back then, and eating was still a challenge.

"Okay, no rush. Just be honest and let me know if you don't like it, okay?" Mila didn't ask any more questions, and picked up some rice with her fork and delicately put the serving into her mouth.

The food was delicious and, thankfully, Mila chatted throughout the meal, while Aria fell into the pattern of picking up the food with her fork and putting it into her mouth. Soon, her plate was empty and Mila was beaming. When the meal was finished, Mila looked at her.

"Tell me the truth. Are you on a diet?" The comment hit Aria in the face. It took a moment to respond.

"No. Not really. I…um…I just try to watch what I eat.

So I eat slow…and well, I don't want to put on weight."

"Weight? Girl you are thin. Seriously, I don't know you that well yet, but maybe too thin."

"Oh…well, thanks!" Aria had fought the urge to run to the washroom and heave the garlicky dinner into the toilet, but she focussed on Mila's warm eyes and felt gratitude. She shifted subtly in her seat, trying to push aside thoughts of the food sitting in her bulging stomach, as Mila chatted about something. Aria concentrated her neighbour's eyes, her full lips, and tried not to stare at the bump in her throat.

Since then, Mila continued to cook and invite her over, and Aria ate slowly, loving each bite but more, loving the fact that her new friend never mentioned her weight or her eating habits again.

As Aria cut into the quesadilla and popped it into her mouth, tasting spicy chicken, sharp cheese, and mango, she realized how far Mila had come from her traditional fare.

"Well, how is it?" Mila's eyes were wide in anticipation, her blue eyeshadow accentuating their roundness.

"Pretty good. The mango salsa is kind of sweet so it offsets the spicy chicken. And what kind of cheese is this?"

"Blue."

"I like it. It works." The comment was half genuine.

"Good. Something to feed my guy."

"Oh…you have a guy?"

"Not yet. But I will find him. Besides we are not here to talk about my dating fiascos. We need to get you to talk to the man in the elevator!"

Aria didn't want to talk about the guy in the elevator. It had been a week and he had not responded to her 'smile.'

"He didn't recognize you. People look different in person. Pictures have no energy, no vibe. They're flat and make you look fat," Mila said, refilling their wine glasses as she blinked at the last word that came out of her mouth.

"I look fat in my photos?" Aria heard the hoarse whisper as it escaped her mouth, her heart starting to beat against her chest.

Mila softened her voice. "No, you look great in your pics. I mean, the camera is supposed to add ten pounds, right? Likely he couldn't place you because it was early, and maybe he was still half asleep."

Aria sighed and waited a moment before responding.

"Maybe, I dunno… He just seemed uncomfortable… and pretty much ran out of the elevator when it opened."

"Girl, it's not all about you. Like I said, it was early and maybe he was late for work or just not a morning person. You don't know. You should have talked to him to see what the deal was. Maybe next time just ask him if he got your message."

Aria's eyes widened. "Well…it was a smile, not a message. Besides, we're boxed into a small compartment and I'm supposed to ask why he didn't smile at me on a dating app? That's too confrontational. No, I can't do it."

"What do you mean a smile? What the hell is that?"

"You know…it's when you send someone a smiley face. You do that first to see if they're interested. If they smile back, then you send a message."

Mila got up, one hand holding the wine glass and the other on her shaking head. "I have only been on an app once and that was the last time." She looked over at Aria and flashed her reassuring smile. "Not that there's anything wrong with those things. But seriously, he will not even see that. Girl, men get so many smiles on dating apps, they can't count them. He has no idea that you are interested."

Aria had never considered that. He may get a lot of smiles. He was a cute guy after all.

"Maybe…maybe, I should send him a message."

"Okay then." Mila refilled their glasses again. "Want me to help you write it?"

Aria blushed and shook her head, while Mila giggled and started talking about her day at the nail salon.

Mila's mom, Eva, had moved to Toronto after leaving an abusive husband in the Philippines. She had come over with two of her sisters and they'd rented a small, three-bedroom apartment in Parkdale. Mila grew up with three female cousins and they'd all shared a bedroom until her tenth birthday. Then she moved to the couch because, at that time, everyone called her Eva's son.

Eva had worked in a high-end nail salon in the Philippines and was famous for her creative nail designs. She quickly found a job working in a salon in Parkdale, doing nails and mopping the floors after the shop closed. After a few years, the shop owner decided to call it quits, after having been in the business for thirty-six years, and move back to Hong Kong with her husband to retire.

Eva's older sister Esther was an accountant and together they bought the salon business with the money they had been saving all those years living in the cheap, Parkdale apartment they shared with the odd cockroach. The shop itself had not been renovated in years. The sinks and chairs were in useable shape, but the bathroom tiles were cracked and the linoleum floor was peeling. Every step was dangerous, Eva feared. What if the tiles were rotten underneath and someone fell through the floor? Esther decided to call up their rich, second-cousin, Martin, who lived in a big house in Mississauga, near the lake. She asked him if he wanted to invest, or help out with repairs and they would pay him back. He chose to give them a loan so they could hire someone to change the floors and repair the bathrooms.

Eva and Esther cleaned and painted the interior

themselves and made some esthetic changes to upgrade the place, but not too much.

"Remember, we are in Parkdale," Esther said. "Customers don't expect a fancy salon like in Rosedale. They won't feel comfortable and they'll go to Shauna's on Bloor."

The sisters decided to keep the name of the salon, which meant they didn't have to buy a new sign. Mitizi's Nails was theirs.

Mila had grown up in the salon. Although at that time, she was known to everyone as Eva's son Milo. Every day, after school, Milo would stop by and hang around with his mom until she was ready to go home for dinner. He liked watching women get their nails done. The transformation from old, cracked, and peeling, to vibrant, shiny, and new fascinated him. He was intrigued by the tiny flowers his mom painted using a miniscule paintbrush and his eyes gleamed when she glued rhinestones onto the tips of the nail like tiny, diamond tiaras. Sometimes, he imagined himself with long nails, painted hot pink with a rhinestone on each tip. No flowers. That was too much. The subtle bit of bling was just enough flash, so when he waved his hands, the stones would catch the light and send a shimmer through the room.

He never asked his mother to paint his nails. One time, she asked him to throw out a bottle of polish that looked empty. Seeing a bit of colour at the bottom of the bottle, Milo kept it, and from then on, he checked the garbage cans for old bottles. Using some of his mother's thinning liquid when she wasn't looking, he poured as much as he could out of each bottle into one, and formed his own colour mix. After cutting and filing his toenails just the way his mom did, he covered each one with the deep shade of pinky red. Milo was careful to do this during the winter so he could cover his feet with socks without looking suspicious. On evenings, he would pull off his socks and lie in bed admiring the glamourous toes, imagining that he was lying on a beach in the Philippines.

As he grew older, his mom let him work in the shop on weekends for pay. He swept the floors and took out the garbage. Sometimes, she was too busy to prep the ladies, so he would greet, seat, and help them choose colours and styles. Not all the women deserved the rhinestone crown though. He was careful to suggest the accessory to a few of the nicer ones, who tipped well and treated his mom with appreciation.

His mom worked long hours in the shop, with only two employees to help. They were useless, in Milo's opinion. Felicia with her cell phone in her ear all the time doing half-assed work, and Marva who was caught stealing from the cash register. She begged to keep her job, saying that her husband wasn't working and she needed to feed her kids. Milo's mom took pity and kept her on for another month, until she saw the new leather jacket in the back room, stuffed in a shopping bag and shoved in a corner.

Marva left in the spring, so Milo offered to help at the shop full-time for the holidays so his mother could take her time hiring. She reluctantly agreed, saying that he should get a job that he liked and not spend his days messing around with women's feet. But she taught him how to do a pedicure and he became so good that he started getting repeat customers and referrals.

Suddenly, the shop was buzzing with rich ladies wanting pedicures every week, with the rhinestone tiaras, as Milo branded them.

One day, Milo was scrubbing Mrs. Liu's heels when she looked him right in the eye and said, "You gay?"

"Huh?" He was startled.

"Only gay boy do pedicure. Your mom know?"

Mrs. Liu lived in Forest Hill and her husband owned a manufacturing company in China. He was rarely home and she was alone most of the time. She got a mani-pedi every week and said that she wanted to look pretty when lying around her pool in the backyard all day.

"I'm not gay." Milo scrubbed her heels harder, looking for a callus.

"Look at me." The command was harsh and he was forced to look up. "I don't care if you like boys or girls. You just need to be honest with yourself. My boy is gay. I love him all the same. I just ask if your mom know. You tell her. Okay?"

Milo nodded and was silent for the rest of the pedicure. She didn't push anymore and gave him a $50 tip.

It was the second time anyone had asked him that question. He was sixteen years old.

He had always been attracted to other boys. In gym class, he looked at the other boys in the changeroom and felt a little stir inside him. Sometimes, he would get an erection and hold his towel or a shirt in front of him as he ducked into the washroom. His mother asked him about girls at school and he talked about the blonde that had pretty hair, but he really liked the Filipino girl the most. The comment made his mother beam with pride and she nudged him to ask her to invite her home for supper. Truthfully, he wanted to know how the blonde styled her hair so that it caught the light just the right way to make it shine. And the Filipino girl wore the best jackets. Funky, stylish, retro. He often wanted to ask her where she shopped. He was certain it was one of the vintage shops in Kensington.

Oh, and her skin! It was the same colour as his and yet there were no zits, no blemishes. Did she wash it every night like he did? How did it not dry out?

So he wasn't really lying about his interest in these girls.

Not really. His best friend was a girl but a different kind. June. She was in his class and they ate lunch together. Her hair was short and she wore glasses, jeans, and hoodies. Milo often wanted to suggest some mascara to make her eyes look a bit bigger, but he wasn't sure how to bring it up. June was a tomboy, his mother said when she came for a barbeque one Saturday afternoon.

June told Milo she liked girls one day when they were sitting on the steps behind the school eating lunch. She said she always knew, even as a little girl.

"Do you like girls or boys?" She posed the question right after her confession.

"Huh?"

"You heard me. Girls or boys? I don't see you hanging out with guys very much or playing sports. You're always at your mom's shop doing nails."

"I just help her out. She doesn't have a lot of help."

"What about her employees?"

"They aren't that good."

"Well, it's okay with me if you like boys. Or girls. I don't care."

That was the first time someone had seen through him. When Mrs. Liu asked, he had felt exposed, naked. How did they know?

He came out to his mom a year later. She said she'd suspected it when he started bringing his friend Alex home after school and they went down to the basement for hours. "I knew you couldn't be playing video games all the time," she said. Then she wrapped her arms around his frame and squeezed him, whispering in his ear, "Please be careful." When she let go, her head turned quickly, but not before he saw the tears in her eyes. He wanted to ask if she talked to Mrs. Liu but it seemed unnecessary at that point.

Alex was his first love and the relationship had lasted

until they graduated from high school and then Alex's parents sent him away to university. Milo stayed at home but went to college to learn proper beauty techniques at his mother's insistence. Only when he'd earned his diploma would she make him part owner of the shop.

It all seemed very easy and Milo figured the secret he'd been holding inside was out and it didn't matter to anyone. He could like boys and that was that. But when he graduated from beauty college, and began working at the salon full-time, he felt a stirring inside. Every time he looked in the mirror and saw the stubble on his chin, he cringed. He hated the sight of his naked body but he wasn't sure why. All he knew was the more he worked around women, the more he coveted their skin, their breasts, the way their pants hugged the curve of their hips. At first, he figured it was from watching too many soap operas in the shop. But the feelings only got stronger, until he had to question why he so wanted to be one of them.

Seven

Rob slipped into the chair and thanked the hostess. She responded with a giggle and tucked a piece of hair behind her ear before backing away, turning, and making her way back to the foyer.

He checked his phone, which said 5:12. Miranda said she would meet him at the bar. The bank was a haven for gossip and if they left together after work, rumours would be circling the entire tower by the next day, like dirt from the streets caught in a wind tunnel.

Rob was surprised when she'd asked him for a drink. She was one of the new lawyers at the bank, and when she appeared in the empty office that morning, the buzz went through the workplace like a thunderbolt.

"Hey, did you check out the new lawyer in Hector's old office?" Dimitri was standing in front of his desk, peering over the half wall that was supposed to provide privacy. Rob hated when people did that.

"Nope. Haven't been around that way." He continued typing.

"Oh man. You have got to get out of this cubicle and move around. She. Is. HOT!"

Rob's fingers paused and he looked up. Dimitri held eight fingers up over the wall. He grinned and walked away. Rob got up, coffee cup in hand. If he took the long way around, he could get to the kitchen by passing her office.

The lawyers sat in glass offices in one corner of the floor. When the company moved locations three years ago, they decided to jump on the open-concept bandwagon. But after the employee survey showed that ninety-six percent of the staff were opposed to an open concept, the leadership team decided to compromise. The office would be open but each desk would have walls that would provide privacy when employees were sitting. The legal team insisted they worked on confidential files and made sensitive phone calls, so they were given glass offices like the executive team. The walls muffled the voices, but everyone could see when fingers were inserted into noses and crotches were scratched. It was like being inside a car. Everyone felt they were hidden.

Rob made his way across the floor, turning right to take the long way around. When he came close to the glass offices, he noticed the one with a gold name plate that read Miranda Cole was empty. Maybe she was in the washroom, he thought, and continued to the kitchen. As he turned the corner, he suddenly met green eyes.

"Oh. Sorry."

She was holding her mug away from her body.

"That was a close call." She smirked and walked around him. He turned to see the back of her head as she made her way down the hall to her glass office. Muscular calves lengthened by heels. He always liked the way a woman looked in heels. Tanya wore really high heels all the time.

"Well, did you get a good look?" Dimitri was eating the daily lunch special from the cafeteria. Butter chicken over what looked like noodles. Another fusion creation.

"If she's the woman that I ran into in the hallway, yeah, she's attractive."

"Kick-ass legs, right? Looks like she works out. Maybe a kickboxer." Dimitri finished chewing and swallowed before continuing. "And a lawyer. That's a lethal combination."

"Yeah, it would be." Rob tried to brush off the conversation.

"Have you seen those calves?"

Rob shrugged and changed the subject. He saw the way she looked at him when their bodies crashed into one another. He'd felt it.

In the afternoon, they met again in the kitchen when Rob was washing his coffee cup.

"A man who does dishes. Gotta love that." Her voice was husky on some words.

"I do them all the time." He wasn't sure if he sounded defensive or flirty; he avoided her eyes.

"Really? You might be one of the few that doesn't leave his cup in the sink for someone else to scrub. I mean, just look at these discarded, dirty cups." She gestured at the mugs in the sink and a few sitting on the counter, left hours earlier as the coffee stains dried and crusted.

"I see them. But how do you know that they've been discarded by men?"

She put one hand on her hip and cocked her head to one side. There was that smirk again but she looked a bit sheepish. She said nothing and he smiled.

"We didn't get properly introduced when you almost ruined my suit with coffee. My name is Miranda." She held out her hand.

Rob grabbed a paper towel, wiped his wet hand, and took hers. She grasped his firmly and squeezed before shaking it.

"I'm Rob," he managed to say.

"Lovely to meet you, Rob. What department are you in?"

"Digital banking. I'm the manager of digital."

"Ah, very nice. Well, I hope to see you around again, Rob." And she turned and walked away, her heels clicking on the ceramic floor.

They had flirted for about a month before she asked him for a drink. It was nicely timed with his breakup from Emily. Dimitri was convinced that she was interested.

"Man, she's always walking by your desk with that look in her eye."

Rob saw it too. Sometimes she came into his cubicle and leaned over to see what was on his screen and brought in a subtle scent of vanilla or something like baked goods. Sometimes her breath smelled like coffee and he felt like turning his head to lick the inside of her mouth.

During their kitchen encounters, she made a point to stand very close to him. Once, she'd reached over and smoothed his hair, saying it was sticking up and did he wake up late that morning? "Were you out late the night before?" she asked as he felt heat pass over his face.

Some days, she walked straight past him without a smile. Just a slight nod of acknowledgement, and continued facing straight ahead. Eyes like green glass.

He couldn't ask her out. Her position made him her subordinate. She worked with the CEO of the bank. He was just a middle manager sitting in a half-walled cubicle.

On Friday afternoon he was finishing up a brief, hoping to sneak out by 4 p.m. to meet his friends for drinks at the local bar downstairs. She'd appeared almost silently, and he caught her scent before turning his head to see her leaning on the edge of his desk.

"You look very intense." Her voice was low; her eyes were shining. He moved back a little.

"Just doing my job," he said, not sure how else to respond.

She threw back her head and laughed. "Yeah, you seem to do your job well. Anyway, I'm heading out of here early. Friday afternoon and the sun is out. Join me for a drink."

Rob paused for a moment, trying to process the question. "I've got a bit more work to finish up...but sure."

"How about the Plaza. Rooftop."

"Okay, that's around the corner."

"How about five?" She didn't wait for a response. "See you then. Don't be late." And she turned. He watched her walk away in those high heels that made her teeter ever so slightly.

But by 5:22, he was still sitting alone and without a drink. The patio of the Plaza was open all year round, heaters warming the guests who drank overpriced martinis and admired the infamous skyline view.

Rob wanted a beer. He looked around for the small bowl of almonds that were usually on tables at the upscale bars. But then he remembered that after the pandemic, shared snacks were no longer permitted.

"Hey handsome. Waiting long?" He heard the husky voice on 'handsome' as she slid into the seat in front of him and placed her coat on the back of the chair.

"Hey" was all that he said. She sat down, emitting a slight waft of perfume.

She giggled. "Sorry I'm late. I was held up by Brad. He has no concept of Fridays or weekends. I wonder how his wife deals with it."

"Yes, that sounds like Brad." The word felt foreign on his tongue. Rob never called the CEO by his first name. In fact, he never had to address him at all.

"He's a workaholic...but I guess that's his job. I'm sure his wife is happy with the compensation."

Miranda requested a wine list and scanned it over before suggesting they order a bottle. Rob usually drank beer in bars as wine prices were pretty high, but he didn't protest.

The waitress uncorked the bottle of California red and poured a small bit into the glass in front of Rob. He looked over at Miranda's expectant face.

"Would you like to do the taste test?" he asked. "Since it was your choice."

"No, you go ahead."

Rob tasted it. It was similar to the wines his mother often served with dinner. He nodded. "It's great."

When the waitress left, Miranda lifted her glass. They clinked and he took another sip.

She talked and Rob listened. After graduation, she got an internship in the government and was fortunate to be offered a full-time job at the Ministry of Finance. It gave her great experience, but after ten years, she needed a change. The bank was an opportunity to work in the private sector and move up.

The waitress returned to refill their glasses when Miranda started asking Rob about his career. He didn't really want to talk about work. His job managing a team of people who worked on the website wasn't especially interesting. In comparison to hers, his job didn't seem like a career. His only decisions were simple executions of his VP's instructions. He kept his description brief and turned the talk back to her while she ran her foot along his leg under the table. She must have removed her shoe because he could feel the softness of her toe from under his pant leg.

By the time they got into the elevator to leave, his head was spinning. Funny how he could drink three beers and feel warm and relaxed, but wine was different. One glass made his muscles relax. Two and a half made his world fuzzy.

As soon as the elevator door closed, he felt the crush of her lips. The wine tasted better in her mouth. They made it downstairs to the lobby of the Plaza and she called an Uber. "You paid for the wine" was her rationale. "What's your address?"

The Uber made it down Bloor Street in minutes. Miranda held him in lip-lock the entire ride and when the car stopped, the driver cleared his throat a few times to get their attention.

Rob avoided the eyes of the concierge as they made their way down the hallway. Miranda's heels clicked on the ceramic floors and he suddenly wondered why she wasn't wearing winter boots.

A few people were waiting for the elevator when they rounded the corner. Miranda whispered something in his ear and giggled. The door slid open and she pulled him inside, asking him what floor to push. Once the door closed, she started kissing his ear, and Rob realized they were not alone.

In one corner of the elevator stood a woman with a ponytail. She was staring straight ahead. Even in his half-drunken state, Rob could tell she was uncomfortable. Her lips were pursed and she was fiercely focused on the buttons of the elevator. She looked familiar and his mind told him to pull back from Miranda but, somehow, his body would not cooperate. A *beep* indicated they had reached his floor; the doors slid open. Miranda grabbed his hand and yanked him as she jumped into the hallway. Rob looked back as the doors closed and met the woman's eyes. She looked upset.

Eight

"They were pretty much making out in the elevator." Aria heard the hysteria in her own voice and took a deep breath.

"What did she look like?" Naomi asked, her voice sounding a bit hollow, which meant she was on speaker phone.

"Black hair…skinny, three inch heels. She had him cornered so I didn't see her face. He saw me though. I'm sure of it."

"Hmm." Naomi paused for a moment in her more-than-usual calm and rational manner, reserved for when she was trying to control a situation. "Well, he's a man and, if a woman is throwing herself at him, his brain is occupied and focused on one thing."

It was true, Aria realized. What was he supposed to do?

"That's true. But it means he's dating someone."

"Or it could have been a one-night stand." Naomi's voice softened a little.

"Either way, he's with someone else."

"At that moment he was with someone else." Naomi was back to her matter-of-fact demeanour.

"Well...the thing is...he hasn't responded to my 'smile' and he didn't seem like he cared that I was in the elevator while he was making out with that woman."

"He's a man. Sex was around the corner. Besides, you haven't even talked to him."

"I know. I'm just saying that he's with someone."

"At that moment he was."

"He could have been a bit more discreet."

Aria waited for a response but heard nothing. Then water running.

"Sorry, I had to pee. What were you saying?"

"Nothing. I'm just nattering, that's all," Aria said, picturing Naomi walking around her house with her sleek headset, checking the mirror, peeing, washing her hands while the phone sat on the kitchen counter. "It doesn't matter anyway. He's just a guy I see in the elevator all the time."

"Have you gone out with anyone else?" Naomi asked.

"From the app? No. I haven't really looked."

"Well, I asked Mike about some of his friends but he hasn't gotten back to me yet. You need someone who works at the bank. A professional."

"Yeah...I know, a guy with money. Well, let me know if Mike knows anyone but, honestly, I am in no rush. I only joined the app because...well, I'm not sure why I joined. It was just there on Facebook. Listen, I'm going to make some dinner. We'll talk later, okay?"

She hung up and sent Mila a text.

Saw the guy in the elevator with another woman. Making out.

Mila texted back right away.

Nasty. What did she look like?

Aria had lied to Naomi. She'd taken a good look at the woman when they were all waiting for the elevator. Wearing sweatpants and a T-shirt, her hair pulled into a ponytail to keep it away from her face, she had just gone downstairs to check her mailbox. Two women were in the lobby debating if they should take the elevator or run up the ten flights. Finally, one convinced the other to take the stairs to burn off the cannoli they'd just eaten from the bakery down the street.

Rob's eyes looked glassy and the woman was kind of hanging off him. He didn't seem to notice that anyone else was standing in the lobby and Aria wondered if he was drunk. His hair was sticking up at one place when the woman ran her hands through it.

She was a smidge over his height. Stilettos that stretched her muscular calves, and a flat bottom uncovered by a short, silver down bomber jacket. Her short hair was slicked back and her lips were stained from wine and smudged lipstick.

When the elevator door opened, the woman pulled the guy inside and leaned into him. They didn't push the button so Aria hit 14 and 17. She could hear the giggling from the woman as she buried her head into the light-haired guy's neck.

Aria stared straight ahead, thankful that the mirrors only lined the side walls of the elevator and not the front door. For some reason, her eyes always went to the mirrors when she entered the elevator to make sure her hair was in place. When people were inside, she resisted the urge to look. Once, she wasn't thinking and checked her hair in the mirror, only to have one woman say, "You look beautiful," which drew laughter from the others in the small space and made Aria feel stupid, and a little vain. She wasn't sure if the woman was being nice or sneering. So she said nothing in return and stared at the buttons on the chrome panel.

The buttons were a poor distraction. Lined up neatly on the chrome panel, they offered little in the way of interest. Each one was a perfect circle that went from grey to red at one push. Aria envisioned them as red Smarties. Although she'd never liked the red ones because, for some reason, they always tasted bitter in her mouth. Instead, she preferred the pink and sometimes the yellow. What if the buttons on elevators lit up in different colours instead of only red? What if each floor was assigned a colour so people associated their floor with a colour. But then again, were there enough colours in the palette for thirty-five floors, minus the thirteenth, of course.

The elevator needed something on the door to keep people's interest as they brushed shoulders with strangers in an uncomfortable silence. Perhaps a daily quote or a poem that gave everyone a lift to start their day. As the couple beside her smacked lips, she realized for the first time that there was no music playing overhead. She needed music right about then; even a song that she hated. Instead, she was trapped inside a small, silver box, avoiding reflections, staring at bitter, red Smarties and trying not to think about the couple making out beside her.

When the elevator stopped at 14, Aria watched the light-haired guy and the clingy woman exit, and just before the doors slid closed, he turned and their eyes met. For a second, she thought she saw his eyes widen, like when a light switches on in someone's head. But the doors shut him out and she was being taken up to her floor.

She texted Mila: *Skinny white girl. High heels, short black hair.*

Mila: *Was she hot?*

Aria: *Seriously?*

Mila: *Fuck him. move on.*

Aria: *I know.*

Mila: *Maybe he only dates white girls.*

Aria: *Maybe.*

Aria opened the freezer and picked up the carton of Heavenly Hash ice cream. There was one scoop left and she ate it out of the container with a spoon.

Tyler didn't let her keep ice cream in the freezer. The first time he saw the carton in her shopping bag, he picked it up and questioned her. "Ice cream, Aria? Do you know how many calories are in one scoop?"

"I know...but it's my only treat. I'm allowed to have one."

"Are you serious about getting fit or not?"

They had only been dating a year at that point and she laughed it off, took the carton and placed it in the freezer. She told him that she would only have a scoop as a treat now and again.

He ran a couple of miles every evening after dinner and ate only vegetables and meat. Once in a while he ate a scoop of quinoa or brown rice.

They met on the waterfront trail one Sunday afternoon in the fall. She was making another attempt to start running and had just crossed the Humber Bay Bridge, heading west, and had slowed down to catch her breath and walk for a minute. A tap on her shoulder made her turn to see a cute guy holding a tissue packet in his hand.

"I think you dropped this." He was smiling.

"Oh...yeah, that could be mine. Must have fallen out of my pocket." Aria's one nostril had a habit of leaking every time she slowed down. She felt it happening as she reached for the tissue.

"Are you okay? You seem a little winded." He looked concerned but she wanted him to leave so she could wipe her nose.

"Yeah...thanks. Just catching my breath. I'm only just starting up again." She pulled a tissue out of the packet and managed to catch the drip before it rolled down to her mouth.

"That's good—a new start. You know, you can run for five minutes and stop for five and then go again until you build up momentum." He sounded like he knew what he was talking about.

"Oh yeah? Thanks...that's what I've been doing."

"Good for you." And he stood there, not moving, not going on with his run. He was tall. Maybe six feet. And had sandy brown hair. When he smiled, a dimple on his left cheek made him look boyish. "I'm Tyler, by the way."

"I'm Aria."

"If you like I can run with you a bit. It's always helpful to have a running buddy."

He was cute in a boyish kind of way. Aria continued to wipe her nose and sniffled a little.

"Sure…that would be great."

They ran for five and stopped for five until they reached the Mimico Bridge and Tyler suggested an iced tea at Starbucks. She didn't notice that he frowned a little when she ordered an iced coffee with one sugar.

He texted her a few days later for an official date—a running date.

So they met at the Humber Bay parking lot early on a Sunday morning. Aria showered before the date, even though she would have to take another one afterwards. She was a bit skeptical of sweating in front of a guy on a first date, but she figured cleaning before would eliminate any potential body odour. Not that she had much body odour anyway, or maybe she just didn't notice.

Tyler was standing in the parking lot waiting when she arrived. He seemed taller this time and he was wearing black Adidas running shorts and a snug grey T-shirt. His arms were lean and muscular and his pecks showed through the shirt. Her stomach flipped over a couple of times and she became immediately self-conscious. He was really fit….and she was just starting to get back into running. What if she couldn't keep up?

But his wide grin was reassuring and he coached her through the run. They ran for five minutes and then walked. After an hour, he suggested a coffee at Starbucks and Aria felt her stomach grumble. Why not brunch, she thought. Smoked salmon eggs benedict was floating through her mind, but she didn't suggest it. Later, she realized that if she had, there wouldn't have been a second date.

Aria was surprised at how quickly the relationship had taken off. It seemed easy at the time, until she reflected on it later. She was enamoured with the lack of head games. He was open about his feelings for her and his intention. When he first saw her standing beside the Humber Bay Bridge, gasping for air, her bangs moist from sweat, he found himself drawn to her. The tissue falling out of her pocket was the signal to follow the inclination.

The fact that he only took her for dinner once during the courting phase seemed a bit odd. Naomi was more vocal about it than Aria.

"He's only taken you out once?" Her tone was judgemental.

"Yeah. He's a health nut and doesn't like to eat out."

"Where did you go?"

"We went to The Keg. He likes the fact that you can order a protein and vegetables. No carbs."

"Okay, well that's not bad. But only once seems strange. Maybe he's cheap?" Her eyes had narrowed then as if she was drawing a conclusion. "Well, if that's the case then you need to move on." She leaned back in her chair and Aria could see the wheels turning in her head. Then Naomi leaned forward quickly to ask the next question, which was anticipated. "Who paid for dinner? Don't tell me he made you pay half?"

Thankfully, he hadn't and Naomi breathed a sigh of relief at Aria's quick response.

"So what about the other times? What do you guys eat when you're together?"

"We've gone for lunch after a run." Aria was fearful at that moment, knowing that Naomi was already forming an opinion about Tyler. She was afraid to tell her that, often, they just parted ways after a run.

"Where does he take you?"

"A local place near Humber Bay or wherever we are running."

"What do you eat?"

"He eats anything that is not greasy and doesn't eat carbs. Mostly he orders salads. He likes avocado and eggs."

Naomi had rolled her eyes. Aria was becoming slightly annoyed at the amount of questions and judgement, but she knew it came from a good place.

"Okay, well, it's not ideal. I mean at this point he should be wining and dining you and cheating on his diet to make sure you're happy."

The words resonated with Aria. But she tucked them away inside her mind and focused on the big picture. Tyler was a good guy. He had a good job as a teacher and he was socially aware. He didn't know much about people from the Caribbean but he wasn't racist and he believed in social justice. Most of the kids that he taught were ethnic and he often talked about their progress. He cared about making sure that each one had a chance.

No one was perfect. He didn't like eating in restaurants and was health conscious. Not a deal-breaker in Aria's mind, and Naomi's expectations were too high sometimes. That's what happens when someone is brought up with privilege and can demand what they want in life.

So despite Naomi's questions and narrow eyes of judgement, Aria allowed herself to fall into a relationship with Tyler.

At the time, she was thirty-one; nine years from forty, when childbearing became risky. Or so her mother kept saying. "Some women c'yant get pregnant afta forty. Chandra had three miscarriages and the doctor said she was too old to carry a child. That is why she only have one." Her mother always brought up her older sister, Aria's Aunt, who got married late and ended up with a man who cheated on her. Chandra moved to the States and eventually came out as a lesbian, but only to Aria. Her parents pretended not to know, and she only visited home once every few years, so her daughter could spend time with her grandparents. She never brought her partner.

When Aria told her parents she was moving in with Tyler after six months, she saw the look of relief on her mother's face.

He was a good-looking man, though not the kind that would make you stare when he walked into a room. But the kind that grew on you and became more appealing as he talked. His body was fit, lean, muscular. Aria still had her flat stomach and shapely butt, which was dangerously prone to getting bigger if she wasn't careful, he used to say with a laugh. Later, Aria realized that those weren't jokes.

"You're beautiful. But you know, as we get older, our metabolism slows down and it's harder to keep the weight off. If you start building lean muscle now, you won't have an issue with it later."

They worked out regularly. She hated running because it bothered her knees but Tyler told her she would get used to it. Her body was groaning from underuse. He coached her until she could run 5k without stopping. She started getting very hungry and craved carbs but their fridge was stocked with fruits and vegetables and, after the ice cream incident, she dared not bring sweets into the house.

One day Carmen brought in a cheesecake that she'd made for Fazia's birthday. Aria eyed the dessert longingly and when Carmen handed her a plate with a thick slab of cake covered in strawberry topping, she shook her head.

"What, you don't like cheesecake?" Carmen seemed offended.

"Um...yeah I do but I'm trying to watch my sugar intake."

"Sugar intake? Diabetes?"

"Um...no, just trying to watch what I eat...you know."

"Girl you are getting skinnier and skinnier by the minute. What does your handsome Tyler think? Men like women with a little booty."

Carmen moved the cake closer to Aria's face until she was forced to take the plate and once that happened, it was too late. She inhaled it, relishing every bite. It was the best cheesecake she'd ever eaten.

But after it was over and she was back in her cubicle, panic set in. Tyler had texted her to say hi while she was eating the forbidden food. It wasn't even food really, she could hear his voice. He knew.

The vomiting wasn't because she ate the cake. That's what she told herself. It was because she felt sick. Her stomach was churning. Maybe the cream cheese was bad. Maybe she was developing a dairy allergy.

But she threw it all up. She had to. The nausea was overbearing but since it would not come out on its own, she had to give it a little push. Her fingers down the throat tickled just the right spot to make her stomach heave and relieve herself of the dairy and sugary strawberry concoction. Ugh. Creamy going down, slimy coming up.

A few swishes of water got some of the vomit taste out of her mouth and Aria made it back to her desk, a little guilty. Although she wasn't sure why.

The next time she induced vomiting was after an over-indulgent dinner with Naomi, who insisted on trying out the new chicken and waffles place that opened in Port Credit. She tried to order a salad, but Naomi was having none of it. "You made me drive all the way out here so you could order a salad? No way. If I'm breaking my diet, so are you. Fried chicken and waffles soaked in maple syrup."

It was delicious. Just like everyone said. Even when Aria's stomach said "no more," she managed to find room. It took everything in her to refrain from licking her plate.

Later, she excused herself and went into the washroom. Both stalls were occupied and one woman was waiting. She lined up and tried to control the panic that was rising in her. Or maybe that was the chicken and waffles and maple syrup churning in her stomach and climbing back up. Seconds felt like hours and she shifted from one foot to the other.

"You really have to go, huh?" A woman with a pink pixie cut and heavy black eyeliner looked at her curiously, her pupils large.

"Um…I just feel a little queasy." Aria stopped shifting.

"Okay, you can go before me." The woman half smiled.

She couldn't vomit while a woman was waiting outside.

"It's okay. I can wait."

The stall opened, and the candyfloss lady shrugged and disappeared inside. Whoever was inside the other stall had not yet come out. Aria felt sweat trickling down the sides of her body. Tyler would hear if she threw up at home. Then he would ask her what she ate. She couldn't lie, so eventually it would come out. And then he would be angry that she'd listened to Naomi and ordered an unhealthy dinner of two thousand calories. It would make him dislike Naomi even more.

Lucky for Aria, both women emerged from the stalls at the same time and she pushed her way inside one of the tiny cubicles. Putting two fingers deep inside her throat she forced the meal to come back up. What went down sweet came up slimy and vile. She washed out her mouth twice with water and made her way back to the table.

When Naomi asked if she was okay, Aria explained that the mix of wine and syrup had made her stomach queasy.

Naomi shrugged and took a sip of her wine.

Months later, she would follow Aria into the washroom one evening and listen at the door.

Spooning the last bite of ice cream into her mouth, Aria remembered why she didn't buy maple walnut anymore. She tossed the cardboard container into the garbage and made a mental note to buy another one the next time she was at the grocery store. Maybe two.

Mila was still texting.

You ok? You need me to come down?

Aria responded. *I'm ok. It's no big deal.*

Ok. Eat some ice cream and sleep well. And forget him.

Nine

Rob's leg hurt. He opened his eyes and saw the ceiling. It took a few seconds for his eyes to focus and for his brain to determine where he was. His room.

He wondered if he was dreaming about the leg, but when he reached out with his hand to move the heavy object that was making it numb; he felt a body part. That's when he turned and saw half of her face in the pillow.

The memory came back and he realized it was the sexy lawyer from the office. Black hair covered her eyes and her mouth gaped open. He moved the covers a little and saw the pale white skin. Her leg was flung over his, pinning it down. Heavy.

Rob shifted his body and tried to ease his leg out from under hers. He couldn't really feel it. Suddenly, she moved, releasing his limb as she turned over.

He got up from the bed and felt the pounding in his head. Hobbling over to the washroom, Rob splashed water on his face and reached into the medicine cabinet for an

Advil. He pushed it down his throat by drinking water from the tap with his hand.

Bloodshot eyes, headache. Hangover. He stood in front of the toilet and recalled the incidents from the night before. They met at the bar. They had some drinks. They came back to his place. She kissed him in the elevator? They had sex… loud…she was on top of him, her hair in front of her face, hiding her eyes as she put her head back.

Argh…the pounding in his head told him to stop thinking. He flushed the toilet and headed back into the room. She was sleeping on her side in a fetal position, her butt sticking out and her feet curled under her. He watched her for a moment before slipping under the covers and closing his eyes. The Advil needed to kick in.

He must have fallen asleep again because the next thing he knew, she was performing oral sex on him. She stopped for a moment and looked up at him with eyes blazing. Before he knew it, she was on top of him and his head no longer hurt.

When it was over, she jumped off the bed and disappeared into the washroom. He heard the toilet flush and, a few minutes later, she emerged and began gathering her clothes.

"Want some coffee?" he asked, watching her slide into her pants.

"Can't do coffee today. Gotta run." She walked over to the bed and pressed her wet mouth on his. He watched as she grabbed something that was sitting open on the chair—her bag—and walked out of the room calling behind her, "Great time. Call me."

He was a bit relieved. He didn't like talking in the morning.

He put the grounds in the filter and flicked the switch to turn the machine on. Then he picked up his phone and clicked on the dating app. The red flag indicated fifteen messages. The yellow icon said thirty-six smiles.

He couldn't see the messages because he wasn't a paying member. Maybe he should go through the smiles while he waited. He started clicking.

***

Miranda was in her office early Monday morning. On his way to the coffee room, Rob saw her walking back down the hallway, probably to her office.

He thought about Friday night. They'd had a good time, but he wondered if it was a good idea since he was her subordinate at work. She was the legal counsel after all, so she would be aware of the rules. Rob smirked at the last thought, leaned back in his chair, and checked his emails. He wanted to see her.

Their paths didn't cross all morning and when lunchtime came around, he had a quick thought about popping in to say hello and see what she was up to for lunch. Then he remembered again why it wasn't a good idea. Grabbing his jacket, he walked down the hall to the elevator and passed one of the small meeting rooms. Through the glass, he saw Miranda sitting at the table with the CEO and the CFO. Her eyes flicked slightly as he passed by and then she turned her attention back to the men. She was working.

By 6 p.m., Rob decided that he had done enough for the day, logged off, and grabbed his jacket. As he entered the hallway, he looked straight into Miranda's green eyes.

"Hey," she said, with a toothy smile. "Haven't seen you all day. Where have you been hiding?"

"Hi. It's been a busy day. We had a few customer issues over the weekend. Mondays are all about troubleshooting." Small talk. He was done with work for the day and didn't want to spend any more time on unnecessary chatter.

"I figured you were busy and didn't see you in the coffee room. But hey, Friday was fun. We should do it again sometime."

Rob looked at her. She was an attractive woman in an intimidating kind of way. Black suit, high heels, red lipstick. He thought about the Robert Palmer video from the '80s.

"Sure. That would be great. Let me know when your schedule is free." His voice was casual but he felt a flutter in his stomach.

"I'll do that for sure," she said with a coy smile and walked past him.

Ten

The date was set at a coffee shop in Bloor West Village. Sunday evening. Aria found street parking on Runnymede and made her way over to the venue. She thought about walking but the temperature had dropped way below zero, and the walk would take her at least twenty minutes. Runny nose and windblown hair wasn't her ideal date look.

When she approached the café, silhouettes of people perched at tables became visible under the dim lights. Busy.

There was that feeling in her stomach. Not butterflies. They couldn't cause such a ruckus. Not even knots. Just that inexplicable feeling that made her nauseous. Like she'd felt the last few months of her relationship with Tyler when she had to take her clothes off in front of him.

As she scanned the room, she noticed a man sitting alone at one of the tables. He looked a little older than his photos, but they were pretty accurate. Aria walked a little quicker and as she neared the table, he stood up, a wide grin revealing two pointed incisors that were longer than the rest of his front teeth.

"Aria?" He pronounced it "Ar-eye-ah."

She corrected him.

"Oh sorry. I'm not really good with names that are different."

"It's okay. I'm the same way."

They ordered coffees and fell into a conversation. He was an architect for a medium-sized firm in the city. He liked binge-watching Netflix shows and was halfway through *The Office* for a second time. As he talked his teeth looked sharp. Aria wondered if he could bite someone's neck and give them two vampire holes.

"What's your favourite place for dinner?" He was looking directly at her. Aria was afraid to answer in case he was going to suggest dinner.

"Um… I don't really eat in restaurants much."

He sat back, disappointment flooding his face.

"Do you like to cook instead?"

"Um…not really."

"So then what do you eat?"

The lie came easy. "Cereal mostly. I can boil eggs, too, but that's only on special occasions."

The date lasted one hour and Aria thanked him for the coffee and headed back to her car. The streetlights were on and a handful of people walked along the street. Bloor West was always a quiet community.

As Aria drove into her parking spot in the underground garage, she craned her head to the left to see if the light-haired guy was in the area. It had become a habit to check if he was walking from his parking spot in the back and heading toward the elevator. He wasn't. This time, she felt relieved.

She locked the car and headed to the doors, realizing that the guy from the coffee shop never posted photos that showed his teeth. His smiles were always closed-mouth.

Aria touched her fob to the security panel and the door clicked open. She was trying to picture the guy from the *Vampire Diaries* when she looked up into blue eyes.

"Hi." The light-haired guy was looking directly at her.

Aria said nothing. For what seemed like a minute, they stared at one another. Finally, she opened her mouth and forced the greeting out. "Hi."

She faced the elevator doors. Noises indicated that the elevators were moving but the red light on the button was unwavering.

"Cold outside?" he tried again.

"Not really." Aria stared at the red button, willing it to go off.

"My name's Rob, by the way. I think we've run into each other before."

Aria turned her head to see his extended hand. His hair was short, neat, sticking up a bit on one side as if he was scratching the side of his head all day. He wore a navy down winter jacket and jeans. On his feet were tan winter boots. She reached out and touched his hand before pulling it away. "Nice to meet you."

The red button was stubborn.

"I didn't get your name." He was relentless.

"Aria." She forced herself to look at him. She saw uncertainty.

"Great to meet you, Aria."

The red button died and the elevator chimed. Aria marched forward, impatient as the doors slowly slid open to let her inside.

She pushed 17 and 14.

The air stood still for a moment.

Heat washed over her face as she stared at the two lit up red buttons. There was no way to make them go out.

"Thanks…." It was almost a question.

Aria turned and looked directly at him. "Um… I remember it from the other night."

"Oh." He looked confused.

"Yes. You were with someone. A woman. And you asked me to push the button for the fourteenth floor." Why did she say that he was with someone and why did she lie about pushing the button for his floor? He had never asked. Aria smiled, as if she was standing in front of Tyler after gaining ten pounds.

"Oh, right. Yeah, okay. Good memory." He still looked confused.

The elevator stopped and Rob stepped out. Once in the hallway, he turned and smiled. "Good night, Aria."

The doors closed.

***

"You pushed his floor? Haha!"

Aria didn't get off on the seventeenth floor. She went straight up to Mila's apartment and banged on the door. It was only 8 p.m. Mila was in her robe.

"I only have a little bit of red left." Mila poured half a glass of wine and placed it in front of Aria, who was sitting on the stool in front of the kitchen counter. "He didn't remember you from that night." Mila wasn't asking a question.

"I don't think so. He looked kind of embarrassed when I said he was with a woman. But he just seemed dumbfounded by the whole conversation. Like he had no idea what I was talking about. I bet he doesn't even remember."

"He was drunk, lady. You know it. They were going upstairs for some booty. He probably picked her up from the bar. That's nothing." Mila laughed.

Aria sipped the wine. It tasted like it had been opened last week but it felt good going down.

"His name is Rob."

"He looks like a Rob. White." Mila's wine glass was almost empty. "He does not remember that night. He. Likes. You."

Aria stared into Mila's face. "Why do you say that?"

"He introduced himself, didn't he? Men don't do that to just anyone."

"Mila, not everything is about cruising."

"Lady, men don't want to be friends with women. They have enough friends. Sex always gets in the way."

The giggles came from Aria first, and then Mila leaned forward, laughing until her silk robe slid open, exposing pink satin boxer shorts with a kitten print.

"What?' Mila said when she noticed Aria's face.

"Are those mine?" Aria blurted out.

"Yours? You think that tiny ass could hold up these large silk drawers?"

"Silk?" Aria raised one eyebrow and looked Mila in the eye, as the two immediately burst into laughter.

"I have that SAME PAIR of polyester satin-like undies! I think you saw mine and were jealous!" Aria couldn't stop giggling.

Mila doubled over and Aria flung herself onto the couch, and together they laughed until their eyes watered. It really wasn't that funny but Aria felt good and safe with Mila.

When she went back down to her apartment, Aria let herself embrace the giddiness. Maybe he did like her.

***

Mila studied herself in the mirror. When her robe had opened and Aria saw the silk boxers, her first instinct was to grab both sides of the robe and pull them around her. How much did Aria see anyway? Until she decided, if she decided to have the operation at some point in her life, she was still a little shy about her body, especially in front of cis people.

Since the two had become friends, Mila had felt a comfort level with the petite woman she'd never experienced with anyone else. Aria never made her feel like anything but a girlfriend. Still, Mila didn't want to freak her out—reality could be a game changer for some cis folks.

The boxers were really comfortable and the looseness of the material around her body was freeing. She imagined the feel of pure silk next to her skin but, until she could afford those, the satin-like ones would do for everyday use. *Polyester*...she grinned at Aria's comment.

The black-and-pink lacy panties she bought in large at The Bay were saved for dates. Men liked to lift her dress and see sexy underwear and they knew what was underneath. Women stopped to admire the style, rub the fabric between two fingers, and check out the look from the bottom before slipping them off. Mila hated them. They were itchy and uncomfortable and she hated buying large. The boxers were better, but no one ever saw her in those. Except Aria now. As Mila stared at her body, she recalled how Aria was more concerned about having the same pair, and the shock from seeing anything else was not there. The thought made her smile.

When Mila had told her mom that she liked women's fashion, her mother had laughed. It started with the aprons at the salon. Mila chose the pink ones to the customers' delight. Then she started wearing open-toe shoes to reveal the painted toenails. The clients giggled, admiring her work and asking for the same.

"It's good to show what you can do," her mother would say.

Mila followed her taste, purchasing items from the women's racks at Winners. The sales clerks were indifferent, eyes flicking to her manicure as she swiped the debit card.

By the time Mila was in her early twenties, her hair was long; silk locks inherited from her Filipino genes. She wore it loose when she wasn't working in the salon, loving the feeling of the strands flowing down her back. The middle part reminded her of Cher in the '70s, and she often stood in front of the mirror, practicing the tuck behind one ear. Her pants were tight and she had a fondness for oversized blouses.

"You dress like me when I was young," her mother would say with a laugh. "In the '80s."

Her first pair of high heels were bought at the clearance rack from the Winners on College Street. By that time, the older lady who worked the changerooms knew her.

"Here, try them on inside," she said, ushering Mila into privacy. Behind the safety of the door, Mila tried on several pairs of heels and pranced around the small room as much as it would allow. Her feet were a size 10 women's, so there were always a couple of pairs on the shelf and in the clearance section back then. But in the past ten years, the larger sizes became more scarce in the stores as they became more noticeable on the feet of women and cross-dressers at parties in the Village.

She'd bought the gold strappy sandals first. They had two-inch heels and her plan was to practice in her room before debuting them publicly. The second pair were more conservative. Black flats with a pointy toe. Good for work.

As she slipped the flats on at the front door of the apartment, her mother appeared, bag on one arm, ready for work.

"Ano ba! What are those?" Her mother reverted to Filipino expressions when she was stressed. She stood in the entranceway, her forehead crinkled in that exaggerated way it would if Mila were offering her a plate of fried pork with potatoes instead of rice.

"My new shoes," Mila said proudly, her heart beating against her chest.

"They are girls' shoes."

"Yeah, but I like them."

Mila's mother looked her directly in the eye, as the hard line of her mouth softened. "Your toes are not displayed. The women will want to see your pedicure."

"Well, maybe I can do a manicure then!"

Mila's mother's forehead relaxed a little, but she shrugged. "Bahala ka!" she said, which meant "do what you want"—so Mila took it as permission.

The women in the shop poured compliments over Mila for the entire day. Mrs. Liu whispered in her ear, "I have a pair of open-toe shoes you can have if you like," and pressed a $20 note into her hand. "But they are a small size. Maybe 5."

Mila thanked her for the kindness and agreed that the size was a tad too small.

Later that week, she bought two pairs of sandals for work—both had one-inch heels. One in silver and the other in red. She wore them both to the shop under the wrinkled brow of her mother, who watched the reactions of the customers and threw out Filipino expressions when she felt it was necessary.

Only when they were going to the picnic hosted by the aunts at G. Ross Lord Park that summer did her mother declare her thoughts.

"You should wear running shoes," she said, her forehead smooth.

"I want to show off the pedicure." Mila was sporting a new pair of gold, flat, strappy sandals.

"Those are too fancy." Her mother's voice was the one she used when the customer wanted to pay her for the pedicure next week. She stood her ground and insisted, without emotion, without wrinkles.

"But I bought them for the picnic!"

"Your aunts will be there. Isabelle's grandmother will be there." Her mother referred to her cousin's grandmother on her father's side. An old lady with watchful eyes who spoke no English and was known for her harsh judgements.

Mila knew all too well the reason for her mother's stance. So she went into her room and changed into white Converse runners.

Since then, her mother made no comments about the morph to women's clothing or makeup, except when there were family gatherings, at which Mila was expected to look like a man, even if everyone accepted that she was gay and a cross-dresser. Transgender was not a term that her mother understood.

Christmases were the hardest. Mila wanted to show off with shimmery red dresses and heels. As she got older, she stopped going to the Christmas dinners, often opting to buy herself an extravagant gift instead. And on Boxing Day, she visited her mother and they had a nice meal together.

Her mother never asked her about coming out as a woman. And Mila never told her. She just kept answering to the dead name within the family bubble, convincing herself that they were actually saying Mila through their accents. But it became difficult after a while. Hiding. Pretending. So she began making excuses and stopped going. It wasn't easy, since there seemed to be a family gathering at least twice a month. Tradition.

Her mother protested the first few times, and then stopped inquiring altogether. Mila was sure that she knew and was also sure that her mother wasn't bothered by who she was. But she couldn't imagine how to come out and tell the family. What would she do—make an announcement just before the buffet table was open? Most would be distracted by the race to the food and not hear. Or she could tell them as they perched on chairs around the room, holding the plates in their laps and shovelling food into their mouths. The vision of judgemental Uncle Bobby spitting rice onto the floor when she said "Hey, I'm a woman now" made Mila laugh out loud. Although he might use it to distract the family from his affair with his brother's wife. And it could get ugly.

Maybe one day she would muster up the courage to tell her family. She did miss the gatherings.

Eleven

Rob saw Miranda on the app. In her profile picture, she was looking right into the camera—green eyes piercing. A slight smirk on her face. The photo made him smile as he recalled the memory of their 'date'.

Since he was no longer a paying member, he could only see profiles. Women were really bold in their photo choices. Some were wearing lingerie and bikinis. There was even a woman in the shower, showing the side of her wet body. Something about the picture put him off.

Miranda's profile name was Legal Eagle. He read her profile and found a cleverly written self-description that alluded to sex without really saying it. Her photos showed various scenes: outdoors straddling a bike and wearing a baseball cap, another in a black dress, showing off her long legs. They were carefully chosen. A wide assortment that showed her varied interests. She was strong and exciting and probably smarter than most of the men who dared reach out to her on the app. What was she doing there in the first place, he wondered.

The profile intrigued him and Rob wanted to see her again. This time, he wanted a few less drinks so he could get to know her a little better.

On Tuesday, he ran into her in the kitchen. They jumped into conversation, as they had in the past before the date. She smiled at him and laughed, even touched his arm at one point. He suggested a drink later. She said she'd go back to her desk and check her daily schedule. "There might be a late meeting today; I'm not sure," she said.

He worked until just after 6:00, and the pangs of hunger gnawing at his stomach told him it was time to end the work day. There was no message on his phone, so on his way out, he walked down the hall and took a quick peek around the corner of her office to find that the lights were out. Not tonight.

The subway was packed. The combined voices of hundreds of passengers became white noise and he let his mind wander to Miranda. She must have been busy with work.

On Wednesday, he saw her in the hallway as she came out of a meeting. A quick nod and smile in his direction and then she turned into the women's washroom.

By Friday, he was so immersed in work that he didn't think about anything else. His mother called a couple of times with demands for his next dinner visit. He tried to see her once a month or so, but lately she had been asking about his dates and there was one conversation where she'd hinted about a woman she wanted him to meet. He told her that work was keeping him occupied.

Friday night he met his colleagues for drinks at the bar. He ended up taking an Uber home, and when he woke up the next day, he had another headache.

It wasn't like university. Hangovers at middle age took a couple of days to wear off. Rob spent Saturday on the couch, nursing his throbbing head and drinking water, telling himself that it was the last time.

By Sunday night, he had finished the leftover rotisserie chicken and potato salad in his fridge. There was nothing left to eat except frozen burgers in the freezer. But he had no bread. Rob toyed with the idea of eating the burger plain but opted to head over to the grocery store down the street.

He piled his cart with multigrain bread, chicken fingers, a steak, apples, orange juice, salad mix, granola bars, potatoes, and a carton of eggs. The cashier smiled at him and blushed when he approached. As she scanned his goods, her blue eyes moved back and forth from the register to him. She couldn't have been more than twenty-one. Probably a student, he thought.

As he placed the groceries into the trunk of the car, Rob noticed the older lady from his floor. She was pulling her small grocery cart out of the store. It was filled up to the top and she seemed to be struggling. The night air was cold, so Rob approached and asked if she wanted a lift. The wide eyes stared at him in fear. She stepped back. She didn't recognize him.

"I live in your building. On the fourteenth floor."

As his older neighbour squinted at him from under the wool toque, recognition washed over her face. Then a smile. But she shook her head.

"I like the walk," she said. He watched as she pulled the cart across the parking lot and down the sidewalk. At that point, he wished he had walked. What was he doing driving two minutes to the store?

By the time he got back to his building, his stomach was growling. Tomatoes. He forgot tomatoes. As he unloaded the car and walked to the elevator lobby, he saw her car pull in. The woman from the pool.

He waited in the elevator lobby a minute. When he saw her nearing the entrance to the lobby, he pushed the button, knowing the elevator would take some time before it arrived. One was usually broken or being serviced.

Rob pulled his phone of out his pocket and swiped to check Facebook. He rarely posted, preferring to be an observer. It's funny how people seemed to get suddenly brave when safely behind their computer screens. As if they didn't have to run into others in real life after they'd posted something racist or sexist.

He glanced sideways, seeing her figure step through the doors and enter the lobby. When she stood beside him, he caught a waft of coconut.

He turned and greeted her. She seemed startled, her eyes wide, and said nothing for a moment. It seemed like minutes until she mumbled something back.

He tried again. This time something about the weather. She responded without looking at him. Maybe she was having a bad day. But it was Sunday evening and she was wearing makeup.

The elevator was taking its time, as he had anticipated. He asked her name. She mumbled it hesitantly.

"We met before..." it was more of a question than a comment, when the doors slid open and she sprinted inside.

He reached to push his floor, but 14 was already lit up in red. He waited a moment, wondering if he'd automatically pushed it. One of those moments when you perform an action that you've done so many times, you're no longer conscious of doing it. But then he saw her face.

"From the other night. You were with a woman," she said, her face slightly flushed.

Rob thought for a moment, scanning his brain. The other night? Only when the bell chimed and the door slid open did the memory hit him. She'd seen him with Miranda. That night. Miranda was kissing him and this woman was in the elevator with them.

Once in the hallway he turned and glanced back. He wanted to say something more, but what? His voice had its own idea and he heard himself say, "Goodnight" before the doors closed.

Did he meet her somewhere else? Then he remembered—the app! His mind raced and once inside his apartment he put down the groceries on the floor and checked. He had forty-eight more smiles. Rob clicked through for ten minutes. She was the one on the dating site who'd smiled at him. The one from the swimming pool with the big eyes. The one who saw him making out with Miranda the other night.

A memory flashed through his head: the look on her face when he'd stepped out of the elevator with Miranda. Rob felt a pang of regret, wondering if he should have been more mindful when he saw another woman was in the elevator. He hated when couples made out in front of people like that.

A rumble from his stomach reminded him about what he was supposed to be doing. As he got up from the couch. A notification sound filled the air. It was a text. From Miranda.

Hey lover. Long time no talk. I missed you the other night.

Rob dropped the phone on the coffee table and walked into the kitchen. He pulled out the frying pan, sprinkled some Montreal Steak seasoning on the steak and, once the oil started to smoke, he seared the meat on one side, remembering to turn on the fan above the stove. The patio door also needed to be open in case the heat from the pan set off the fire alarm. It had happened often and the older lady down the hall had rapped on his door to ensure he wasn't burning down the building.

What did Miranda want? She'd ignored him for the entire week. He felt like an insignificant cog while she pranced around in her suits and high heels in closed door meetings with the CEO. Now she wanted to play?

The steak bled onto his plate, meeting with the salad. The colour reminded him of Miranda's lipstick. It had been on the collar of his shirt the next day and he'd had to take it to the dry cleaners.

Rob cleaned up and went back into the bedroom and picked up the phone. There were two more text messages from her. Two photos. The first of her lying in bed in a silky robe, the belt loose around her stomach. The second was a selfie with pouted lips as if she was sad about something.

He switched the phone off and went to his fridge for a beer. He was getting too old for games.

Twelve

The second guy was worse. He must have been about ten years older than his photos and he kept clearing his throat when he talked as if there was a large mass of phlegm lodged there. Aria could barely keep down her coffee.

The third date was better. His name was Anthony and he sported a two-day beard that he preferred to keep that way. He didn't like the full-grown, hipster bearded look. He was from Guyana and he also had an Indian name—Adesh.

"My brother's name is Nathaniel Narine and my sister is Amanda Anandi. But she uses the Indian middle name as her first. She thinks we should all be using our Indian names instead of trying to be westernized," he explained.

Aria liked him right away. Honest, easygoing, and he'd asked to meet for a drink instead of coffee. The conversation over the drink went well and he suggested staying for dinner. They ordered chicken fajitas for two and laughed about the silly things their parents told them about white people.

"Like how they only cook hotdogs for their kids." Anthony laughed as he piled grilled chicken and veggies into a wrap and topped it off with guacamole and some shredded lettuce.

"Oh, you're not having any cheese?" Aria asked.

"Nah. I'm not a big fan of cheese. It's saturated fat, and I try to keep my fat intake down."

The words stopped Aria just as she lifted the last bite of chicken, cheese, and veggie-stuffed tortilla into her mouth. Instinctively, she lowered her hand and put the piece back onto her plate. He didn't seem to notice.

Anthony ordered more drinks and the waitress removed their plates with Aria's last bite of quesadilla left on hers. He talked about growing up in Guyana and moving to Toronto when he was ten. Scarborough, he said. That's where they lived in an Ontario housing townhouse complex. His father was a teacher back home but couldn't find a job here so he went to work in a factory while he took a few night courses. His mother worked in accounting as a payroll clerk and, after a few years, when his father got a teaching job, they moved to their own house just a few blocks away.

He worked as a financial analyst at one of the mutual fund companies downtown. Naomi would be pleased that Aria found a finance guy. The evening ended late. Anthony walked to her car and they parted with a kiss on the cheek.

"Let's do this again," he said. And she nodded.

Mila had already texted by the time Aria reached upstairs.

What happened? Is he still there?
No, we had dinner and he went his way.
You didn't invite him back to your place?
I did, but he's gay.;)
Send him my way.
I thought you only dated straight men.

I'm fluid.
He's nice.
Nice is boring. Is he hot?
He's handsome.
Sounds boring.
Night Mila.

Anthony texted the next morning, saying he had a good time and did she want to go to the movies this coming weekend. Aria read the text and put down her phone. She'd had a good time on the date but there was an ongoing argument in her head about the cheese comment. He wasn't directing it at her, but he was concerned about fat. A little bit of grated cheese sprinkled as a topping was too unhealthy for him.

Then again, maybe there was more to it. Maybe he didn't like cheese or maybe he had high cholesterol and his doctor ordered him to stop eating cheese. Aria wasn't sure what she was feeling. Was she overthinking it? Or was something in her gut telling her to walk away. It took her until the end of the day to respond. She convinced herself that this was not Tyler. And she was not responsible for living up to someone's ideal body image. This was a message that her therapist continued to reinforce. Aria was in charge of her own body, and if she wanted to eat cheese, then she would eat cheese.

Her response to Anthony was simple.

Hey. I had a good time too. Movies sound like fun.

He responded right away.

Great. How about the cinemas on the Queensway? 6 pm, Friday? We can grab a bite afterwards. I can pick you up.

She used to go to the Queensway cinemas with Tyler all the time. The place was always packed and you had to get there early to find a seat, otherwise you'd be stuck in one of the front rows. Once they'd had to sit in the fifth row and she woke up the next day with a sore neck. Tyler told her that she needed to work out more to strengthen her neck muscles.

The date with Anthony was set for Friday and she accepted dinner with Naomi on Thursday. Her friend wanted to be updated on the dating app adventures.

Naomi was craving pizza from the place in Roncy, a five-minute walk from the condo. When Aria pressed the elevator button, her stomach did a sudden flip. What if she ran into the guy in the elevator? Rob.

But it didn't stop at 14. She rode down to the lobby in one sweep. Maybe the other one is fixed she thought as the cold air surrounded her.

November was the month that pushed autumn out and brought in winter, but without the snow. From vibrant and sunshine to grey and cold. Wet cold, dank, and miserable like Gotham City. Filled with dark corners and damp streets.

Luckily, Roncy was a busy neighbourhood filled with hipsters and millennials strutting around in Sorel boots and down coats, hands in pockets, discussing current affairs and climate change. It used to be a Polish and Ukrainian neighbourhood years earlier and the main strip was lined with restaurants that served home-made pierogis and cabbage rolls.

Before she'd moved into the area, the City of Toronto did a revitalization of the neighbourhood, adding bike lanes and encouraging newer businesses to move there. Today it was a mix of old and new. The older Polish couple who owned the shoe-repair shop had been in business for over thirty years. When the community started to change, they'd considered closing the shop and retiring. But their son said it would be a shame to close a successful business. So he took over the shop, making small repairs but keeping the place the same as when his parents ran it. The older lady had told Aria this story herself one day when she was picking up a left boot that needed the heel repaired.

Trendy coffee shops and upscale restaurants snuggled beside independent businesses while the old Revue Cinema held its ground, drawing locals every weekend.

The pizza place was small in a cozy kind of way that one would imagine pizza places in Italy would be. Wooden tables stacked close together with just enough room in between for servers to slide through without touching. The most recent write-up in the local paper boasted of a wood-burning oven and a menu of eclectic, gourmet pizzas and a carefully chosen wine list of Italian vino. That's what caught Naomi's fancy and she'd immediately texted Aria, saying that it had been a long time since she visited her neighbourhood.

Usually, Naomi liked to entertain in her space. 'Holding court' is what Tyler used to say. She loved to be the queen on her throne with adoring subjects she could rule at her whim.

Aria wasn't surprised when he pointed this out. She'd known Naomi for years and the need to be in control was just who she was. When Aria had first moved into the new condo, Naomi visited with a generous housewarming gift and a bottle of Stag's Leap that they polished off in a couple of hours as they chatted on the balcony and watched the street activity below. But afterwards, visits from her friend were few and far between.

"Come to my place," Naomi would urge. "You can stay over. You know we have two extra rooms and I have a cleaning lady, so you don't have to worry."

'Generous' is what Aria kept saying to Tyler. But he insisted it was only because she could be as mean as she wanted on her own turf. No one would challenge her. It was her home, people were eating her food and drinking her expensive wine.

Even before he pointed this out, Aria had observed this behaviour. Christmas one year was particularly obvious.

Naomi had hosted a catered, gourmet dinner and offered her spare bedrooms for the night. Mike invited his friend Will from work, who brought his new girlfriend Simone at Naomi's suggestion. "We'll see if she's right for Will," she'd said. Mike said it was a good idea, but Aria noticed his left eye twitching as he said it.

Naomi was a gracious hostess, and when Simone entered and handed Naomi a bottle of wine as a gift, Aria watched her friend size up the new guest. Simone was stunning. Short, black hair cropped close to her scalp, which accentuated her features. She didn't appear to be wearing much makeup except for mascara, which made her already large eyes stand out. Her dark skin was smooth, her full lips covered with a clear shine. Aria watched as Naomi handed Mike the wine without looking at it, and focused her attention on Will, brushing his shoulder as if dust had settled undesirably.

"Aren't you looking handsome tonight," Naomi had said, giggling. "This must be a new shirt. I don't remember seeing it before."

"Simone got it for me for my birthday." Will blushed a little at Naomi's fawning.

"Well then," Naomi said, and turned and walked into the condo.

The evening wore on with Naomi asking the servers to pour wine from her own bottles. Simone's bottle of red sat on the counter, still in the bag, until Will said something quietly to one of the servers who nodded.

"So Simone, Will tells me that you are a recently published poet," Mike said as he dipped a piece of salmon into the béarnaise sauce before sliding it off the fork into his mouth.

"Yes, I am," Simone replied, casting her eyes downward to her plate and smiling a little.

"That's great! Where can I get a copy?"

"Oh, I have one in my bag. I brought it for you as a gift."

"No," Mike said. "We will buy a copy. A couple of copies if you have them."

"Well, thank you. But I only have one copy on me and I'm giving it to you as a gift for inviting me this weekend." She got up and fetched the book from her bag and handed it to Mike, who immediately started flipping it open.

Naomi sipped her wine and looked around. Aria was fascinated and looked at the cover. "I think I've seen this before. At Indigo?"

"Yes, they carry it." Simone smiled, pride on her blushing face.

"How's it doing so far?" Mike asked.

"It's doing great!" Will said, jumping in. "In fact, the other day, we were having brunch at this new place around the corner from our condo and this woman had the book sitting on her table. We heard her telling her friends how much she liked it."

Simone took a gulp of wine and took over from Will. "She was saying that the poems resonated with her and her life. It was as if the poet reached inside her soul."

Aria watched the pride on Simone's face. Naomi got up from the table, her crumpled napkin dashed on the side of her plate and mumbled as she walked away, "Well, I've never seen it in Indigo before and I'm there all the time."

Aria flinched and looked around the table. Mike smiled and his eye twitched. Will took a sip of wine; Tyler chewed, his mouth a hard line. And Simone was looking at her plate, cutting asparagus before placing the piece into her mouth.

"When is she ever at Indigo? She probably just sends a minion to pick up decorating books," Tyler said when they were going home the next day.

Aria shrugged and said nothing, feeling the accuracy of Tyler's assessment. Everyone had ignored the comment, letting it disappear into the air instead of grabbing hold of it and letting it live. Tyler just couldn't let anything go when it came to Naomi. And the feeling was mutual. But Naomi had been right about him in the end.

Warm smells wafted under Aria's nose as she entered the pizza parlour. She scanned the room, knowing that Naomi would arrive a few minutes late. Aria was early. She liked to arrive a few minutes beforehand to sip water and people-watch.

At her request, the hostess seated her at a small table near the window and Aria checked her phone to see Naomi's text:

Be there in 5.

More like ten, Aria thought. The place was half full, but it was still early. She perused the wine list, trying to guess which bottle Naomi would choose. Sure enough, after Aria had gone through the menu three times, narrowing down her pizza choice and eating almost all of the olives in the small bowl that the waiter had placed on the table, a cab pulled up in front of the restaurant and Naomi stepped out, tossing her head back as the light caught her silky hair.

"Hmm…still not using Uber?" Aria said as her friend sat down at the table, after a kiss on the cheek and a warm hug.

"How safe can it be to get into a stranger's car? None of those Uber guys are trained to drive through the city like the cabbies. Besides, cabbies need to make a living." Naomi took off her coat and was looking around the room when the waiter appeared.

"I will hang it up for you, madam," he said with a smile, his eyes flicking across Naomi's taut body in the black skin-fitting top and skinny jeans.

He returned immediately and Naomi asked for a few minutes to peruse the wine list. The waiter moved away for a bit, but kept his attention on Naomi as her eyes made their way up and down the choices. Finally, she closed the menu and he appeared again. She pointed out her choice and he disappeared.

"So how are you?" Naomi asked, dipping her head a little as if there was a secret between them that had not yet been shared.

"The same as yesterday," Aria said and laughed. The two best friends texted daily, several times throughout the day.

"Yes, well, we have not seen each other in person in about two weeks. You're too busy with your new dating life?"

"Well, work too," Aria replied.

"Work is during the day."

The waiter returned with the bottle of Chianti and two glasses. Naomi tasted, nodded, and he left after pouring two glasses, smiling at Naomi the entire time.

"Let's celebrate," she said, clinking her glass to Aria's.

"What are we celebrating?" Aria sipped the red slowly, tasting the wine she could never order without worrying about drinking away two weeks of groceries.

"The fact that you met someone," Naomi said, smiling her toothy grin of polished, white teeth.

"We had one date. That's hardly worth celebrating," Aria said, wishing she had waited until date three before telling Naomi.

"This one is different. I could hear it in your voice."

"Well, we had a nice date. And we're going out again." This was new information for her friend.

"I knew that," Naomi said, still smiling. She leaned back in her chair, holding the wine stem between two fingers. "When?"

"Tomorrow. The movies."

Naomi wrinkled her nose a bit and shrugged. "Movies. How are you supposed to get to know him if you're sitting in a loud cinema?"

"We will hold hands and let our fingers get to know one another." Aria was used to Naomi's judgements. "If his hands are clammy, there won't be a third date."

Naomi rolled her eyes and picked up the menu. "Let's share a pizza and get something for dessert."

Thirteen

Rob watched the man's head tip forward and then jerk back. Eyes wide, he looked around to see if anyone noticed. Rob averted his eyes and stifled back a yawn. The subway was already full. Sleepy passengers on their morning commute to the downtown core of the city.

He didn't sleep well the night before. He'd dreamt that he was naked in the office and Miranda was laughing at him. Typical cliché dream. Yesterday, he avoided the kitchen except the one time when he had to grab his lunch bag from the fridge, and that sent his stomach into knots. He wasn't afraid of seeing her, he told himself. He just didn't want any more drama or a confrontation at work. In time, everything would cool down and they would run into one another while making coffee and chat like colleagues—or at least like a middle manager does with the company's legal counsel.

The line at Tim Horton's on the main floor of the building seemed to be moving quickly, and Rob took position behind a woman who was holding up her phone in front of her face while she rolled off a couple of sentences in Portuguese. He snickered when he heard "foda-se ele," and could hear the words coming out of Tanya's mother's mouth when she'd told her about their divorce: "Fuck him!"

Large coffee in hand, Rob stepped out of the elevator when it opened on his floor. He saw Miranda's back as she snaked around the corner, heels clicking across the floor. Close call, he thought as his stomach lurched.

On Monday mornings, it took until mid-afternoon for the groggy, dim dust that settled over the office to lift. People walked in later than usual, eyes puffy, hair matted down with water to keep from pointing in all directions, grunting good morning without making eye contact.

Rob gulped his coffee and busied himself with emails. He stifled a few yawns and felt his stomach grumble. But food wasn't on his mind. He realized that avoiding Miranda might simply prolong the situation. They should have a conversation. She was a member of the senior team after all. Legal counsel. He needed to make sure there were no misunderstandings. The last thing he needed was a harassment complaint.

He exited the cubicle with full intentions to march down to her office, only to see Miranda walking down the hall with the CEO beside her. Her eyes flicked to his and, without recognition, flicked away again as she continued talking.

Throughout the day, Rob got up a few more times with the intention of running into her in the kitchen or the hallway. He even passed her office once. But she wasn't around. An all-day meeting perhaps. Finally, he responded to her message.

Hey. How's it going?

Clearly she was busy so he figured the response would come later in the evening. But suddenly his phone buzzed.

Meet me for a drink tonight. 6:30 at the bar.

He looked at the clock. 4:23. He was hoping to leave by 5:00.

How about 5:30? He wrote back.

Can't. Meetings.

He didn't want to wait around, but wanted to figure out what she wanted. So after a few minutes, he responded, *Ok. See you later.*

She was ten minutes late. Rob had already ordered a pint when her figure appeared, slowly making its way in his direction, her red lipstick visible from across the room.

"Long time no see lover." She kissed him wetly on the mouth and slid into the other side of the booth.

Rob smiled but no words came to mind.

"How are you?" Her voice was like corn syrup.

"Keeping well. How about you?" He kept the smile on his face despite the annoyance that was building up inside, ready to erupt. Did she have a split personality? Suddenly a thought struck him. Maybe she was bipolar. He looked directly at her and the fire that was growing inside him diminished.

"Well, I am good. Very busy at work these days." She leaned over the table and put her hand on his arm. "I'm sorry I have not had time to stop in and chat. We are going through some issues with this case."

"Oh?"

"Yeah, sorry. I can't really talk about it. But it's been tense lately. Some days I just want to walk out and never go back."

Rob wasn't sure what to say.

"I see…" was the best he could do in that moment. He looked up for the waitress and when she caught his eye, he gestured.

"I didn't want to burden you." Miranda kept talking. "But I know I've been neglectful. I sent you pictures though. So you wouldn't forget me." Her voice was sugar. Rob smiled and they ordered drinks.

***

Someone was playing organ music. Rob opened his eyes and didn't recognize his surroundings for a moment. He sat up in the bed and stared at the room. Black curtains allowed one beam of light to fall across the bed, cutting him in half.

Miranda came flying into the room, fully dressed, her hair wet. She grabbed her phone and the organ music stopped.

"Sorry about the alarm. I usually get up before it goes off. I gotta get in to work. Early meeting. Can you close the door behind you?" And in a flash, she left the room.

He threw back the covers and sat on the edge of the bed. A pile of clothes on the floor took him back to his university days. Waking up in a strange bed, searching around for shoes, only to find he had to get a cab back to his own place and had no idea where he was.

It wasn't a memory he wanted to relive. He was the website manager for a national bank, sitting in the legal counsel's bedroom on a work morning. Embarrassment spilled over him and Rob waited for a moment before getting up to make his way toward the door from where Miranda emerged. He assumed it was the bathroom. It was.

He made his way to the mirror, noticing how his hair was standing in all different directions. He splashed water on his face and tried to rub off the lipstick mark on his neck. It wouldn't come off. Maybe it was the kind you could wear all day. Emily used to say it was the only kind she'd wear.

Using soap from the black dispenser on the counter beside the sink, Rob tried to remove the mark. The soap made it sting and he leaned into the mirror and looked closer, touching it. Slightly bumpy. It was a bite mark. The memory came back to him.

Rob peed and went back to the bedroom to gather his clothes. The sunlight coming through the window was stronger and he pulled the curtain aside to see the street below. Tiny people were buzzing around what appeared to be Bay Street. Shit, what time was it, he wondered.

He searched through his pant pockets for his cellphone and found it had only one bar left. It was already 7:30! He had to get home and get ready to come back downtown for work. The office tower must be close by. Running into one of the guys from the bank would not be a good idea. There was enough juice left on the phone to call an Uber, but what was the address?

The thought of going straight to work was an idea. No one would notice he was wearing the same clothes from the day before.

Rob dressed quickly and made his way down the elevator, closing the door behind him as Miranda instructed.

She lived on the thirty-first floor. The elevator arrived and he stepped inside next to an older woman in a wide brim hat and holding a tiny dog. He called the Uber after getting the building's address from the concierge and within minutes he was on his way home, his mouth filled with the sour taste of alcohol after not brushing the night before.

As the driver made his way down the Gardiner, Rob recalled the events of the evening. After one drink, he'd looked into her steel eyes and began the conversation. He enjoyed their time together but, because of their work relationship, they needed to remain friends and nothing more. Her eyes became liquid and, somehow, she managed to convince him to have another drink. Then he agreed to one last night together. Her toe was in between his legs under the table and he decided it wasn't such a bad idea. One last time. He remembered the elevator ride in her condo building. She was kissing his neck. She wanted to have a quickie in the elevator and he remembered his pants being unzipped. Heat spread over his face at the memory. This wasn't where he wanted to be.

The Uber jerked to a stop and Rob saw the front of his building. He mumbled a thank you to the driver and slipped him a ten, even though he was supposed to tip on the app. The guy had made it to his place in record time and Rob would have time for a shower.

Fourteen

Secretly, Aria agreed with Naomi about movies on the second date. It seemed so high school. He should have thought of something more creative. Plus, she wasn't thrilled about having him pick her up either. Aria decided she would text Anthony and ask him to meet her at the theatre. No explanation was necessary.

Is everything ok? He texted back.

Yes, fine. I have an errand to run after work.

Ok, I can pick you up earlier and take you to your errand.

It's ok. I'll meet you there.

He didn't text back for twenty minutes. And then it was, *Ok.*

By the time Friday night came around, Aria's head was aching. A dull pain that made her head feel stuffed up, groggy, like when she slept in too long in the morning and woke up disoriented. She pulled on a pair of jeans and a sweater, put her hair into a ponytail, and applied lipstick. She could hear Naomi's voice as she pulled her bangs out from the ponytail to sweep the side of her forehead. "You look like you're going to the gym. Why don't you let your hair down?"

She shrugged off the thought and headed up to the theatre. When she pulled into the parking lot, she could see him waiting just inside the front door. Her stomach flipped over a few times and she felt sick.

Aria parked and made her way up to the building. As she got closer to the entrance, his uncertain eyes met hers and his body relaxed, a smile washing over his face.

"You made it," he said, as she walked through the door that he was holding open for her.

"Oh…you were expecting me to stand you up?" she asked with a sly grin.

"No, I just meant…um…since you talked about running an errand…" He looked at her face and laughed. A little nervous laugh.

"Oh, the errand wasn't a big deal. Just easier for me to meet you here."

He bought the tickets and popcorn and drinks. She declined the candy but he bought M&M's anyway.

Aria didn't pay much attention to the movie. She preferred sci-fi. Anthony didn't ask her what kind of movies she liked. He may have just assumed that chick-flick romance was a given for her.

After noticing that he kept looking over at her during the funny scenes, she made a point to laugh along with the audience. But her mind was filled with the vision of Rob standing in the elevator, his face flushed while the slick-haired woman sucked on his neck. Then he had the nerve to chat her up like nothing happened. "He was drunk," Mila had insisted. "And he was on a date. It's not like you guys are dating. Cause you won't even talk to the guy!"

Mila was a champion for Rob, while Naomi wanted her to pursue Anthony, probably because he worked in finance. But she hadn't met him yet. If there was going to be a 'yet'.

It was Naomi who'd known that Tyler wasn't good for her. She'd started noticing Aria's loose clothing and asked if she was on a diet. "You look good the way you are. Why are you losing weight?"

Aria shrugged it off, saying that she'd begun running with Tyler and the fat was turning into lean muscle.

"Then you should be eating more," Naomi had insisted, her almond eyes cloudy with concern.

"I am eating. We go out to eat all the time."

It was Naomi who'd followed Aria into the washroom that time and stood outside the stall. Aria had grown confident about using the restaurant washrooms to purge so Tyler wouldn't hear.

That evening, after eating every bite of the cheeseburger that she'd ordered at Naomi's insistence, she excused herself as she always did. The music in the washroom was always loud, which worked in her favour. As was her practice, she pushed two fingers down her throat and tickled that spot that triggered her stomach to reject the newly swallowed food. Mashed burger and sweet potato came flying up her throat like a pipe spewing out sewage into the clear water in the bowl. She was used to the taste of vomit in her mouth by that time and wiped her mouth with toilet paper before opening the door and coming face-to-face with a wide-eyed Naomi.

"Did you just throw up your dinner?" Naomi was using that voice she used with Mike when he had a drink with a new female colleague from work.

"Yeah. Must have been something wrong with the burger." Aria was quick on her feet with the response because she'd rehearsed it many times.

"I had the same thing and I'm fine," Naomi said, her mouth stern.

"Well, maybe my stomach is queasy," Aria said, pushing past her friend to rinse her mouth in the sink.

Naomi had watched and waited while Aria cupped the water in her hands and washed out her mouth, using a paper towel to dry herself.

"Are you purposely throwing up so you can stay thin? Aria, that's bulimia." Naomi was never one to mince words.

"No, it's not. Bulimia is when someone binges and then purges." Aria had walked out of the washroom and back to their table with Naomi following close behind.

They sat in silence for a few minutes while Aria sipped the rest of her wine and Naomi stared at her.

"Ari. Listen, you can talk to me." Naomi's eyes had changed. She was the kind Naomi, the one Aria saw when Mike's grandmother died and they had to book last-minute coach tickets so they could fly back to Jamaica for the funeral.

"There's nothing to talk about. I'm fine." But it was too late. Tears sprung to her eyes and Aria wanted to let it out. She covered her face with her hands and allowed the sobs to escape her shaking body.

Naomi said nothing until the tears stopped flowing and Aria's body became still again. When Aria opened her eyes, a packet of tissue was sitting in front of her. And Naomi was silent.

"If I eat too much, I will get fat." The comment seemed to have taken on a life of its own and burst out of her.

"You aren't fat," Naomi said quietly.

"But I will get fat," Aria insisted.

"Who says?" Naomi was going to make her say it.

Aria was silent, wiping her eyes first and then her nose.

"Who told you that you would get fat if you ate too much?" Naomi asked again.

"Oh, well, it's common sense, Nao. People get fat when they overeat."

"You don't overeat. You run four times a week. You're really skinny. Too skinny."

Aria said nothing but looked down at the tissue, blackened with mascara.

"Who's telling you this, Ari?"

The word took a long time to come out. But she had to say it. "Tyler."

Naomi sat back in her chair, her eyes blazing. She knew.

"He makes you starve yourself at home. So when you go out to enjoy dinner, you're worried about getting fat." It was not a question.

"No…he doesn't make me starve myself," Aria insisted.

"I've seen your fridge. There's nothing but vegetables in there. You don't even have a pint of ice cream in that freezer and, Ari, you love ice cream."

"When I was a kid maybe. Do you know how much sugar is in ice cream? It's really bad for me."

"Well, so is Tyler."

The words hit the air like a bolt. Aria said nothing, but lowered her eyes and stared at the table. Naomi said nothing else. She picked up the cheque and they walked out.

Several weeks passed after that conversation before Aria was ready to admit the truth to Naomi. Only when she opened up did Naomi believe that she didn't have bulimia. Naturally, she thought Aria was in denial. But in true Naomi fashion, she had already done some research, likely talked to her father, and realized that Aria wasn't binging and purging like one does when they have bulimia. But she did have an eating disorder.

At first, Aria tried to brush it off. "I'm sure women do this all the time. Regret what they eat and just want to get it out," she said, believing that it happened more than people admitted. Naomi listened with stern eyes and a hard mouth and when Aria was finished, she said the words *eating disorder* out loud while she looked Aria in the eye.

Naomi was all about tough love, and when the words hit, Aria felt a rush of air escape from inside her and she burst into tears. The secret had been like a heavy ball inside of her, and when it became real, the feeling was more a release than a sense of shame and Aria remembered feeling lighter, as if she could lift her arms and fly.

It was Naomi who made the appointment with the specialist. Her father had asked a colleague for a favour and Naomi drove Aria to the appointment. It was Naomi who forced Aria to tell her parents even though she knew they wouldn't understand. Old school, Aria said. The last time she'd seen them, so many months earlier, her mother had said nothing about her weight. She just cooked up a big pot of curried chicken and rice, which Aria threw up in their washroom afterwards. If they'd heard the vomiting, they never mentioned it. Her father had just finished his third beer by that time, and was snoring on the armchair while an Indian movie played on the television.

On the way home with a container filled with leftovers, Aria felt waves of guilt. Her mother took time to prepare the meal and all she did was waste it. She would put the rest in the freezer until she could bring herself to eat it without feeling badly.

Months passed before she mustered up the courage to break up with Tyler. Maybe he would change, she kept thinking. Maybe if she just talked to him about her issue and explained that she just wanted a bowl of ice cream now and again. Would he get really upset? Would he throw away what they had because she didn't want to run ten kilometres every week? Could they go to a restaurant once in a while and eat steak and mashed potatoes? Somehow, Aria knew in her heart that he wouldn't accept what she said. He wanted someone who ate the way he did. He wanted someone who would turn up their nose at carbs and sugar and concentrate on lean muscle and healthy eating. That's who he was. He would never be happy with her and she would always be looking over her shoulder. And miserably coveting ice cream.

Then there was the conversation with her mother. How could she explain that her daughter, now in her mid-thirties, had another failed relationship? And simply because her boyfriend wanted her to be fit. What was wrong with that? She could hear her mother's voice as her father sat in silence. He would just go along with whatever her mother said, so as not to disturb his own peace.

So she waited until after she'd moved into her the condo to tell her parents. Her mother's mouth was stern and she looked away. Her silence was worse than words sometimes. Her father frowned and Aria watched as he opened his mouth to say something. She hoped he would be on her side, reassure her, protect her, but his mouth closed again. Then he looked her in the eye and smiled quickly. It was enough.

Naomi and Mike hired the moving company. They were the high-end movers who came to your home and packed up the stuff for you. "Consider it our housewarming gift," they said.

Now as she sat beside Anthony in the movie theatre, her right hand on her left thigh, too far away for him to reach out and take it, she wondered if Naomi should meet him sooner than later.

***

"Two dates doesn't make a relationship." Mila's tone was lovingly judgemental as usual. They were sitting on her balcony while she smoked a joint.

"Who said anything about a relationship," Aria argued, her arms crossed to keep in the warmth.

"So then why do you want Naomi to meet him?"

"Well…because she has good instincts," Aria said, accepting the joint from Naomi.

"You can't make a decision by proxy, lady. Just because Naomi was right about Tyler does not mean she's some kind of romance psychic."

Aria exhaled. "Yeah, that's true."

"Listen, you are thinking too much. I get it. I mean, we don't want to get hurt. Look at Kurt. After that first night, I was already making space in my closet for him. And how long did that last?"

Aria smiled at the reference to Kurt, the last guy that stole Mila's heart. Turns out, he was married to a woman who allowed him to 'play' on the side, as long as she continued to keep her lifestyle.

"Well, maybe if you had introduced Naomi to Kurt, she would have told you he was married." Aria laughed and Mila smirked before taking another drag.

"So what happened after the movie?" Mila asked. She wanted every detail.

"We went for a drink at Milestones."

"And you let him pay again, right?"

"No…he paid for the movie and the popcorn."

"Girl, men respect women that make them shell out money." Mila sighed and looked at her disapprovingly.

"I don't think that happens anymore. You're living in the dark ages."

Mila laughed. "Did you kiss?"

Aria blushed.

"More than kiss?" Mila's eyes widened with anticipation.

"Wow, you are so nosy. Yes, he walked me to my car and kissed me."

"On the lips?"

"No, on the hand. Of course, on the lips."

"Tongue?"

"No…Just, um…soft."

"Ha! He wants a relationship. Men slip you the tongue when they want sex. They kiss like that when they want luuvv."

Aria said nothing. There was something in the kiss that was not lust. Mila might be right.

When she got back to her apartment, Aria pulled out the half bag of chips from the cupboard and finished them. As she placed the crumpled bag in the bottom of the garbage under everything else, she instinctively found herself walking toward the bathroom. Aria was lifting the toilet seat and suddenly she didn't know why she was there. Naomi's face flashed in front of her and she put the seat back down. Funny how the treatment was never front and centre. Or the doctor's face. It was always Naomi. She was the one who had forced Aria to see the doctor.

"No, I don't need to see a psychologist. You forget that I work in Health Promotion. I know why people purge."

"Oh yeah? So then if you know it's not healthy, why are you doing it?" Naomi was not going to let it go.

"Nao, I've told you so many times—I am not bulimic. I am not binging and purging. I just feel over full when we go out to eat. The portions are way too much!"

It took over a month of her constant nagging. She finally threatened to tell Tyler.

"It's not like he will listen to you," Aria said, trying to sound confident, even though her heart was banging against her chest. "You guys don't even talk to each other."

"He will have to listen. Ari. Do you want me to go that route?" Naomi was hard. "Listen, I am only trying to help here. But if you prefer to keep pretending nothing is wrong, then I will talk to Tyler."

Aria knew it could happen and that there would be a

blow-up. Naomi would accuse Tyler, who would be defensive, and a yelling match would follow. In the end, Aria would have to go home to face him. That would be the worst part. So she agreed to see the psychologist.

After the appointments were set up, Naomi pulled another condition out of the bag. She insisted that Aria tell her parents, which caused another argument.

"Come on, Nao, I already agreed to see a doctor. Now you want me to tell my parents that I am…um…well, I need some help with my eating habits? They really won't understand." Aria looked at the stern-faced Naomi, who sat in the driver's seat of her car, which was parked in front of the hospital.

"You can't even say it can you?" Naomi looked at her. "You are starting treatments for an eating disorder, Ari. Your parents need to know."

Aria sighed and rolled the cuff of her sleeve. "You're looking at it from a different perspective. Your father is a doctor, so he would understand. My mother would not fathom how throwing up could be a disorder. She would see it as behavioural—something I can just stop doing if it makes me sick."

"And your father?"

"Oh, well he doesn't get involved in things like this. And if he did, he wouldn't understand either. My parents are different than yours."

How could she tell Naomi that her parents limited her meals as a child? They didn't want her to end up like Rupa, her father's sister, who was overweight. Aria was actually intrigued by Rupa, whose belly hung over her pants yet who was never hesitant to hide her appetite, despite the obvious looks from the family. She showed up at dinner parties and filled her plate, twice, sometimes three times, and always commented on how good the food was. Some of the younger kids in the family would giggle and comment, while the adult women would look on with amusement, picking at the sparse food on their plates. Once she had to give the young cousins a dirty look for talking about how much the 'fat cousin' was eating.

Then one day in the grocery store, Rupa collapsed on the ground, close to the foot of an old woman who screamed and alerted the manager. A heart attack, the doctor said. It was quick. Later, Aria heard she was clutching a bag of soft cookies, and the thought made her smile.

Even before Rupa died, Aria's father would often comment on her weight. "If yuh eat like that, you go end up like Rupa. Fat. She cyan't even get a husband."

Aria was never allowed seconds. Even when she wanted a second piece of the double chocolate cake her grandmother bought for her thirteenth birthday.

"One piece is enough. You go get too fat." The cake was placed in the fridge and Aria sneaked downstairs that night and ate one more piece, being careful to slice it thin enough so no one would notice. She made the nightly trip downstairs for a few more days until the cake was almost gone.

"Who eat out the cake?" her mother said one day. "Aria? You eating dis cake?"

She lied. There was no other choice.

"No…maybe it was Anand." Using her brother's name was the easiest way out. He played soccer and her parents figured he would burn off the calories.

Naomi didn't know about her parents' rules about eating and Aria wasn't about to tell her now. Who knew where that would lead! Psychology perhaps.

Naomi's body relaxed and she leaned back in her seat. She had only met Aria's parents once, at a Christmas party that Aria threw one year. Her parents stopped in quickly to drop off some cookies and say a quick hello to the guests.

Aria's mother gave Naomi a half smile and offered a meek greeting. Naomi could be intimidating with her polished, upper-crust style and high eyebrows. She was taller than most of the women in the room, which made it appear as if she were looking down on everyone else. It wasn't ideal. The two made small talk, while Aria tensed and found an excuse to pull Naomi away to meet someone else.

Her mother never said much about Naomi after that, even though Aria dropped her name at every opportunity that could lift her image. Her father's profession, the charity work, the fact that Naomi brought a case of wine to the party. Only once did her mother offer a comment. "She seem like a stuck up gyul. But she real skinny."

So when Naomi threatened to tell Aria's parents about the treatments for the disorder, there was little choice. In the end, Aria realized that her friend would not be in the room anyway, so the conversation with her mother, while she was doing dishes in the kitchen, was fairly simple.

"Mom, listen…um…I have to go to the doctor for some treatments. I've been…um…well, I've been having trouble keeping food down and been throwing up a lot…."

"Vomiting? You have de stomach flu?" her mother turned from the sink to look at her curiously.

"Um, no…I'm…um...just not feeling like eating or feeling too full and wanting to get the food out."

"Making yuhself vomit?" Her mother had turned to face her at that point.

"Well, sometimes…"

"So what de docta go do about dat?"

"Well, the treatment is a healthy food plan and group therapy…"

Her mother's eyes narrowed and her mouth twisted. "Yuh have to pay for that? Someone to tell you what to eat?"

Aria shook her head and her mother turned back to

the sink and picked up a soapy dish. "So dat is why the boy leave you." The comment was made under her breath but it hit Aria in the face like a slap. She said nothing and that was the end of the conversation about Tyler and the treatments. She assumed the information would be passed along to her father.

"What did she say?" Naomi asked as soon as Aria let her know that the deed had been done.

"I told her like you asked but she didn't say too much." Aria waited for judgement but it never came. Naomi said nothing and that was the end of the conversation regarding parents and their need to know about her life.

The memory faded and Aria realized she was standing in front of the sink, staring blankly into the mirror. Her eyes used to sit inside sunken holes in her face. Funny how she never noticed it at the time. It was a long time ago. She opened the faucet and let the cold water flow into her hands so she could drink. After brushing her teeth and splashing water on her face, she climbed into bed and picked up her phone. She opened the dating app, went directly to the preferences, and cancelled her subscription. It would expire in two days and she was not going to renew.

Snuggling under the covers, she fell asleep right away.

Fifteen

Miranda didn't talk to him for most of the week. No texts, no discreet visits to his cubicle. When he passed her in the hallway, he got only a nod, sometimes a lift of the eyebrows when she was alone, but never any words and not even a smile. When she was with the CEO, her eyes flicked in Rob's direction, but they were blank. He was a subordinate.

By Friday afternoon, he was feeling anxious. When they met last week, he spent some time explaining why they couldn't continue as they were. But, somehow, he wasn't convinced that she really understood what he was saying. She didn't appear to be listening, as she rubbed his crotch with her foot and ordered more drinks. For some reason, it seemed too easy.

Rob thought for a moment and suddenly realized that Miranda was like Tanya in some ways. She wanted what she wanted and didn't see 'no' as a rejection. She was also a power lawyer. She didn't need coddling.

He looked at his phone. 3:12. Time for an afternoon coffee. The website project would keep him at work for a few more hours and he could use a jolt of caffeine.

The kitchen was empty when he entered and someone had put on a new pot of coffee. As he waited for the coffee to brew, he read the bulletin board. Employee announcements. Upgraded benefit portal. Lunchtime yoga schedule. He'd never tried yoga. Some of his buddies had met their girlfriends at a yoga class. Rob looked at the schedule and wondered if he should check it out. The classes were offered in the gym on the third floor of the building. It was likely that women from the other offices attended. Meeting a woman who enjoyed yoga over drinks was a pleasant thought. He scanned the schedule. Next Wednesday would likely work.

As he pictured himself doing tree pose in gym shorts the thought crossed his mind that maybe he needed to wear something more suitable. But what does a guy wear to do yoga? Suddenly he heard clicks. Like nails on slate, the sound echoed in his ears. He hesitated before turning.

Her eyes were glowing, like his mother's cat when it hid in the bushes beside the backyard bird feeder and took out birds for fun. He involuntarily stepped one foot back and felt his stomach flip.

"Fancy meeting you here." Her voice was smooth.

"Hi." He let out a sigh and managed a half smile.

"Whatchya doing tonight? Meet for a drink?" She was almost whispering as she neared him, the clicks slower, methodical.

Rob looked directly at her and blinked for a moment. His gut was correct. "Oh, thanks but tonight isn't good."

Her eyes narrowed. "Why not?"

Rob stared at the television screen and noticed the bank's VP doing an interview on BNN. He hesitated for a moment before responding. "Last week was fun, but we both agreed that it was the last time."

"Really? We both agreed to that?" She looked at him. Their eyes were locked.

"Yeah, said we should keep the relationship professional."

"Oh, that's very interesting, because if I recall, you were in my bed the next morning." She was still whispering but Rob was conscious that anyone could walk into the kitchen.

"It shouldn't have happened," he said.

A mischievous smile transformed on her lovely face. "Oh right, it's coming back to me now. One last night as lovers. But it's Friday night after all and I don't have any plans. So how about a drink with a friend?"

He hesitated. It wasn't a good idea. He wanted to get up early and go for a swim in the condo pool.

"Well... I am working late. A drink afterwards isn't a bad way to end the week." He couldn't believe what he said.

"Fabulous! I have a meeting at six. I'm sure we'll wrap up by seven. How about the same place?"

Rob wasn't sure why he agreed. He told himself it was just a casual drink and he would go home after only one. He watched the victorious smile on her face as she turned on her heels and walked out. He noticed she didn't get a coffee. She didn't even have a mug in her hand.

Rob stared at the coffee pot. It was full, and the aroma of office coffee filled the kitchen. He immediately regretted saying yes. He didn't want to wake up in her bed after a night of drinking. He could hear Tanya's voice saying he was resistant to shedding his university skin.

"Seriously Rob, you're like the stubborn lizard who's dragging around the old hide!"

He used to laugh at the analogy, especially since she said it with such fire. It turned him on. It used to...and then it became nagging. But she was right.

Rob picked up his empty mug, walked out of the kitchen and down the hall. Miranda never flirted when she sat behind her desk. He would knock on her door and tell her that something came up and he couldn't make it. She would put on her professional face and nod, as if he was saying he would get the website information to her in the morning and he had to leave work due to a personal commitment. As he rounded the corner, the side of the CEO's face came into view. He was sitting across from Miranda and the door was closed. Her eyes flicked slightly but her gaze never shifted away from the man sitting in front of her.

Rob went back to his cubicle. He could send her a text but it was poor form. He would meet her for one drink and they would talk. Nothing more.

Friday afternoons were usually dead in the office. Most people sneaked out early, grabbing their coats from the closet in fly-by fashion and heading directly for the open elevator doors. Rob was alone by 6:45 and he ventured out of his cubicle and looked around at the deserted office space. Snow was falling outside, highlighted through the windows by the street lights. It made little sense to wait around, so he shut down his laptop and grabbed his coat.

The bar was already full but one table at the back of the restaurant was available. Rob ordered a pint and ran his hand over his slightly wet hair. He unlocked his phone and clicked on the icon for the dating app.

A red flag indicated there were waiting messages and he was now up to 242. Although the list was growing daily, he still wasn't interested in buying a subscription. At this point, he wouldn't get through half of them. He checked the smiles, now up to 1084. He scrolled through them, stopping to read profiles of the ones with bright smiles and natural hair. She came up seventh this time. The woman from the elevator. Arielle? Aria. He read her introduction again.

Honest. A great smile. He hadn't seen her since that day in the elevator. He thought back to the conversation. She was so aloof.

Rob clicked on her photo and looked at her smile and her doe eyes. He re-read her profile and recalled the foggy memory of that night in the elevator when Miranda was licking his neck.

He remembered seeing the doe-eyed woman at the pool that day, the sun from the windows reflecting on each droplet of water as she emerged, hair plastered back. She was thin. Almost too thin…

"How are you doing this evening?" The voice jolted Rob out of his memory and he looked up into the eyes of the server and noticed how her black eyebrows seemed high across her forehead as if she was surprised.

"Oh hi. Thanks. I'm good for now," he responded. "I'll order when my friend arrives."

She looked disappointed, as if she had just asked him to dance and he had declined. He watched her walk away in the black spandex dress that stopped just below her rear end. Maybe it was intended to be sexy but tonight it seemed indecent. He watched as she stopped at another table filled with older men in suits. They must have ordered more drinks because her eyes lit up and she scribbled on her notepad.

Rob checked the time on his phone. 7:18. No texts.

He went back into the app and read Aria's profile again and began to imagine who she really was. He passed her car almost weekly and knew that she drove a light blue Honda hatchback that seemed to be a few years old. She had winter tires. He coveted her parking spot, which was close to the garage entrance, and a few weeks ago she was carrying something that reminded him of Woody's. The smell made him go straight to his kitchen and pull out a frozen patty from his freezer for dinner. A meaty sandwich from his favourite burger joint would have been better, but he didn't feel like waiting for Uber Eats or paying the delivery fee.

He scrolled through her photos. She was athletic. A regular swimmer in the pool and maybe a runner. Oh yeah, there it was. A photo of her running, but there was something weird about the smile. Maybe it was just the photo.

Dating someone who lived in the building was risky. As risky as having a fling with the legal counsel at your workplace. But she wasn't Miranda.

He clicked on the subscription page. A few minutes later, he was a one-month subscriber. He put down the phone and made eye contact with the server who sprinted over. Rob ordered a burger with salad and a draft. His phone said 7:38.

When he realized he was stood up, Rob decided to check his inbox for messages while he waited for his dinner. As a non-subscriber, he had seen the red flags indicating messages were waiting, but he couldn't retrieve them. Until now, he hadn't been interested in seeing what he was missing. He clicked on the envelope and started scrolling through the list, pausing on the ones with appealing photos, quickly scanning the one-line greetings, and going back to the list—until one stood out. He stopped. Her smile was unmistakable. And she had sent him a message. Rob was just about to click on her message when the server returned with his burger. Minutes seemed to pass between the plate being placed in front of him and the waiter asking him if he needed anything else. Rob shook his head and went back to the phone. She had sent him a smile and the message over a month ago! He read, and then re-read her words a few times.

He'd never responded. He never knew. And she had been trapped in an elevator with him while Miranda licked his neck. Aw shit! Rob took a swig of his beer and leaned back in his seat. His phone made a sound and he saw a message pop up from Miranda saying a work meeting was keeping her away and she would make it up to him. She had signed with a kissy-face emoji. He signaled the server for the bill, a box for his burger, and didn't wait for change as he pulled on his coat and left the restaurant.

He read the message on the subway ride, when the signal allowed for it. When he got to the condo, Rob looked around the foyer. A few people were waiting for the elevator, their fingers scrolling over their phones. When the door finally slid open, he held his breath, only to see the middle-aged couple from the penthouse emerge. A waft of perfume hit the air as they headed to the front doors where a limousine waited. Everyone in the foyer piled in and he found himself walking slowly, looking behind him, before stepping in while the doors closed.

By the time he was inside his apartment, he'd crafted a response to Aria in his head. He lay on his bed with his phone and began to write. Somehow, the words in his head didn't translate into text. Maybe he could just talk to her in person. She only lived a few floors below him. Perhaps she was already heading down to the pool. He flung off the covers and searched for the new swim shorts he had bought last year. Rifling through his drawers, he found the old Adidas ones with the stitching loose on one of the left stripes. It took a bit of time before he located the new shorts with the tag still attached in a bag in his closet.

***

Rob exited the elevator on the second floor and tried not to run down the hallway that led to the pool. He'd forgotten his towel and had to run back up to his apartment.

He rinsed his body quickly and entered the pool area. He placed his towel on one of the empty chairs and removed his flip-flops before scanning the pool. A toddler was splashing around in water wings while her father stood a few feet away.

Aria was not there.

He stepped into the water and did a few laps, cautious of the toddler and wondering if she had already peed in the pool.

Sixteen

Aria walked out of the changeroom, inhaling the familiar scent of chlorine. She had taken the afternoon off to get ready for her date with Anthony, and figured a swim would calm her nerves.

She walked around the pool, checking all the corners. Except for some dirt settling beneath the blue, there was nothing hiding under the water that would leap up and grab her foot. It was a silly fear. But visions of an alligator being inserted into one of the pool ducts by pranksters filled her mind. She had seen it once in a bad horror movie. The woman was minding her own business, swimming in her own pool, when suddenly, something yanked at her foot. The audience watched in horror as the alligator dragged her underneath the bloody water.

She walked down the tiled steps and felt the lukewarm water on her toes. The management never kept it hot. Or maybe she was comparing it to her steamy showers.

Aria was a strong swimmer, having taken quickly to the water when she was just five. Her mother could swim, but not her father. Back in the Caribbean, her mother went to a convent in town for high school and there was a pool in the yard. "Not like pools here," her mother said. But it was good enough for swimming lessons. She would often show up her cousins when they went to the beach, by swimming out far into the sea. Aria's father wasn't a strong swimmer. His idea of swimming was standing in the water with his friends, waiting for big waves, so they could dive and try to ride them as they crashed down. The one time Aria went to the beach with them on a visit to the island, she'd watched as the men lined up to wait for the waves. Each one stood with arms in front, looking back as the wall of water grew to over twenty feet, and then they would jump just before it crashed. None made it to the top like a surfer, which is what Aria thought they were trying to do. They all ended up close to the sand, looking like drowned rats and gasping for air through laughter.

The pool in the condo was small. Not like the one at Sunnyside, where she could do laps in her lane for a good length without worrying about hitting the cement wall. But it was sufficient for winters, and most of the time it was empty.

She pushed herself off the wall with her foot and put her head underwater. Swimming was like yoga. Her mind focused entirely on her breathing. She had to make sure she blew out the air while her head was in the water so she could turn and inhale when her right arm arched into the air. One missed breath and the entire length was compromised. But she rarely missed a breath.

As her breathing synched with her movements, Aria's body relaxed. She was in a state of hypnosis.

Her arms told her when it was time to get out of the pool. They usually started to do the rubber band impersonation after about an hour. She emerged from the pool just as a mother was leading her toddler out of the changeroom.

Aria smiled at the child, though she suspected that most kids peed in the pool.

As she entered the changeroom, Yellow Flutterboard was emerging from the shower. Her eyes widened as she saw Aria, who sidestepped and entered an empty stall. It had been a few months since the woman had accused her of not showering before entering the pool. And sometimes they ran into each other in the elevator but Aria usually kept her eyes focused on the buttons.

The accusation had been surprising. Aria had emerged from the changeroom and found the older woman in the pool holding onto a yellow flutterboard and staring directly at her, eyes icy-blue. Aria smiled and entered the water.

"Did you see that sign there?" the woman had asked.

"Excuse me?" Aria responded.

"That sign. Do you see what it says? It says: *You must have a shower before entering the pool.*" Yellow Flutterboard's eyes were glass; her lips a hard line.

"Yeah, I saw it." Aria wasn't sure why the woman was telling her about the sign. Maybe she was senile, she thought.

"Well, you didn't have a shower before getting into this pool."

"What?" It was then that she realized what the woman was talking about. "Sure, I did. I always do."

"Oh really? And your hair dried off right away, did it?"

Maybe she was senile, Aria thought, passing a hand over her wet hair.

"Um, I always shower before I get into the pool." Aria was surprised to hear the agitated tone in her voice and watched Yellow Flutterboard roll her eyes and shake her head, before turning away.

As she stood in the shallow end of the pool, wondering what to do next, a woman in the hot tub stood up and looked over, droplets of water rolling off her brown skin.

She had met Aria's eyes and said, "She says that to me all the time."

"She does?"

"Yes, and to my friend here." She gestured to an Asian woman sitting beside her.

Yellow Flutterboard's eyes were wide, her gaze fixed on the side of the pool, her mouth a funny shape.

The water felt cold around her and Aria stepped out, changing her mind about the swim. As she picked up her towel from the chair, through the glass she saw the recreation coordinator, sitting at the desk in the hallway.

Without intending it, she found herself standing in front of the desk, dripping wet, her towel barely wrapped around her body as she explained the situation to the red-haired coordinator, who couldn't have been more than nineteen years old. A student perhaps.

"She's always complaining," the coordinator had said, looking at something on the desk in front of her.

Aria didn't want to point out the obvious. But she'd blurted out the comment. "There are two women in the hot tub who said that she accused them as well. Why does she keep bothering random people?"

"People need to shower before getting into the pool, but she's not the pool cop. I'll talk to the manager," the coordinator was looking down at the desk and shuffling papers, her brows furrowed.

After a week, Aria went back to the pool, and as she slipped into the water, she noticed the recreation coordinator appear to check the temperature of the pool, her eyes focused on her work. Since then, the appearance of the coordinator was consistent, checking the pool's temperature every time Aria entered the pool area.

Aria shampooed her hair and wondered if it was all just a big misunderstanding. Maybe her hair didn't look wet or perhaps Yellow Flutterboard couldn't see that far. She let the warm water wash over her body and applied the conditioner, letting it soak into her hair while lathering soap over her body. The white foam bubbled on her brown skin and her hand ran over the bump of her stomach. She had a tiny belly now. Tyler would be horrified if he saw her.

A few minutes later, Aria was heading to the elevator, wrapped in her bathrobe, wet hair around her shoulders. As soon as she pressed the button, the doors opened and she entered.

***

Aria agreed that Anthony could pick her up in front of the building. He'd made reservations at a Japanese restaurant that accepted bookings two months in advance. But Anthony worked with the owner's sister, so she got him a table within a week.

By 6:30, Aria was standing over a pile of clothes on her bed, wearing only her underclothes. She purposely wore a plain bra and sensible panties so she wouldn't be tempted to show off anything that was sexy in case she had too many glasses of wine.

Anthony never mentioned if the restaurant had a dress code and she didn't ask. Maybe she should just wear black leggings and her high-heeled boots. That was easy, and it could be both dressy or casual. But what if he wore a tie?

Aria ran to her computer and googled the restaurant. The website didn't say anything about a dress code.

By 6:45, she was wearing a black skirt and the black V-neck sweater that called for the circle pendant necklace that rested between her cleavage.

When she got downstairs, his car was parked in front of the building. She hesitated but when he smiled at her from his seat, she opened the door. A pink rose rested on the seat.

Aria's first reaction was to shut the door and run back into the building. Instead, she smiled and picked it up, dipping her head as she slipped into the seat.

"For me?" she said, facing his twinkling eyes. It was the look of someone who was pleased with himself.

"Ah, no, sorry, that was for the concierge...." The comment deserved a laugh and her shoulders relaxed.

"Thank you."

"You are welcome. How was your day?"

Aria never knew how to answer that question. It was the same as "what do you do for fun?" Her day was good at some points, annoying at other times...it seemed like the kind of question you ask when you're trying hard to be polite and have nothing else to say. She responded that her day was fine and babbled for a few minutes about nothing in particular and then asked about his day. This made the ride easier and he talked about the bank and his coworkers and she leaned back into the seat and listened.

He parked the SUV on a side street and Aria offered to pay for parking.

"Ah, no need, I have the Green P app. But thanks."

The outside of the restaurant looked like an abandoned storefront. There was a black-and-white sign, but the windows were covered in paper from the inside. Anthony pressed a button, which Aria assumed was an intercom because a woman's voice answered. He said his name and indicated their reservation and the door clicked. He held it for Aria as she stepped inside.

It looked like any other sushi restaurant in the city. Tables with white linen draped across them diagonally; a sushi bar manned by a chef in a white hat, who seemed immersed in his work while customers perched on bar stools; chopsticks between fingers contributing to the buzz of the collective chatter.

A woman appeared in a black, flowered kimono and helped them off with their coats. Another woman led them to a table in the corner and Anthony pulled out Aria's chair.

There were three selections on the menu. Each selection consisted of a five-course meal but there were no details. Anthony ordered sake and they sipped while discussing the latest Hollywood gossip.

"The chef chooses a daily selection and every day is supposed to be different," Anthony explained. "Are you adventurous?"

She wasn't. When Anthony told her he had made reservations at this popular sushi restaurant, he didn't ask if she liked sushi or not. Truthfully, she didn't hate it, but when Naomi wanted Japanese, Aria ordered tempura.

"Um…I'm on the cusp," she responded.

"The cusp? Of adventurous?" Anthony laughed. "Ah, I think you'll really like it."

Most of the dishes were raw pieces of fish that Aria had never heard of before. Dunking it in soy sauce made it edible, and the pieces melted in her mouth. She had envisioned fishy, slimy, rubbery to chew, but there was none of that.

"You like it." Anthony didn't ask so much as state. He picked up a translucent slice of fish and dipped it in soy sauce before sliding it into his mouth. He had full lips, Aria noted. The stubble on his face had a couple of flecks of grey that looked silverish when he turned his head. She wondered if he resembled his parents. They were probably like hers. First-generation immigrants who ate leftover curry chicken and roti for breakfast and didn't understand how people could pay money to eat raw fish.

"Yeah…it's really good," she said, and meant it.

He picked up the bill, even though she offered genuinely, because she knew it was pricey. But he shook his head and finally agreed that she could leave the tip.

She wanted to invite him upstairs but Mila had already warned her about not giving it up too easy. Besides, her plain, mismatched undergarments would give a bad first impression. "Men don't really care," Mila had said. "But women do, and you will forever regret wearing granny underpants on your first time. And then you'll spend forever trying to convince him that you actually own some sexy stuff."

They kissed in his car in front of her building for a while. Maybe half an hour, maybe ten minutes. The sake made everything foggy. She thanked him for dinner and just before getting out of the car, he handed her the rose that was sitting on the top of the dashboard.

When Aria got into the elevator, her finger hesitated at the button for Mila's floor, but instead she pushed 17. She would talk about it tomorrow.

Aria undressed and lay the clothes over the back of the chair in her bedroom. The beige bra came off and she pulled a faded black T-shirt over her head and climbed into bed. Instinctively, she picked up her phone and clicked on the dating app icon. A pop-up message warned that there was only one day left to change her mind about the cancellation.

The red flag on the mailbox image caught her eye right away. Aria's finger hovered over the phone. She paused. How many messages did she get that were from men she wanted to meet? What were the chances that someone on the app would be more of a fit than Anthony?

He liked her. That much was obvious. The cheese comment was a one-off. She could date a guy who didn't eat cheese. He never told her not to eat it. Besides, Tyler never took her for dinner in fancy restaurants. Unhealthy, he used to say. And who knew what they were doing in the kitchen?

Tyler never bought her a rose either. Maybe it was cultural, Aria thought. Maybe it was her. Maybe she always chose the bad guy who mistreated her because she really didn't want a relationship and it was easier to break up with someone for his many bad traits than it was to justify leaving a man who treated her well. Maybe she didn't want to be the bad one in the relationship. Maybe she was dating her father, who favoured beer and spent his money betting on horse races.

Her mother would love Anthony. Finally, a man from the Caribbean with Indian heritage. Finally, her daughter would settle into a relationship. There would be no more questions from relatives asking why her daughter was not married. The next comments would be "When yuh getting grandchil'ren?" But at least she would have someone in her corner.

Aria closed the app and put down her phone. There was no need to look any further. She turned off the light and relaxed into sleep.

Seventeen

Rob rolled over in bed and grabbed his phone. The app icon said there were messages and he lay on his back to read them. Scrolling through the list, he saw the photos of the women with their pouty lips—one kissing a horse, another hugging a golden retriever. Nothing from Aria.

He had finally responded to her message yesterday evening, after crafting the words in his head as he swam. She wasn't in the hallway when he left the changeroom. Not in the elevator either.

By the time he'd reached his apartment, he knew what he wanted to say. He tried to keep it brief. One paragraph. He hit send and then spent the rest of the day checking.

So far, she hadn't read the message. The app said she was online recently, so why wouldn't she read her messages?

But then again, he realized that he had an inbox filled with unread messages. She must have lots to go through herself. The app could have a better design. Messages that were unread should have a separate box so they weren't missed.

The creators of the app should have another look and do an upgrade, he thought.

Rob got up from bed and decided to go down to the pool for a morning swim. As he descended in the elevator, his heart began to pound. He rounded the corner from the elevator and clicked his pass to get through the doors to the recreation area and headed to the windows that looked into the pool. A quick scan showed a couple of swimmers, but not Aria. She could be in the changeroom.

Rob undressed, showered, and made his way to the pool. The two swimmers were doing the breaststroke, heads above water, legs like frogs, across the water. He eased into the pool and made his way across to the other side. Funny how he lived just a few floors down from her, and yet, their paths had crossed maybe only a dozen times in the past couple of years. Their lives were separated by three floors. She slept above him at night, showered with water that came through the same pipes. He imagined her scrolling through the app inside her apartment alone, just three floors above him, while he scrolled through the same screens, clicked on the same icons. They breathed in the same air in the elevators, walked on the same surfaces. Their shoes shared the same dirt and carried it into each other's homes. There were pieces that touched her that were inside his apartment right now.

"Hey!" A voice startled him out of his thoughts. "Hey, can you move over a bit and give us a lane?" Rob looked up at a man in the pool, holding a small boy.

"No problem. I'm done anyway." Rob was sincere as he made his way over to the steps and climbed out of the pool. He wasn't sure how many laps he did, but his body felt good.

As he waited for the elevator, Rob checked his phone. One text message. He clicked on the bubble icon to see a message from Miranda.

Hey lover. I'm sooo sorry about last night. Work is nuts. I will tell you all about it. Meet tonight for a drink? 9?

Rob was glad that there were no windows in the hallway, because he felt the urge to pitch the phone and watch it break glass. Miranda was playing him, and yet a small part of him wasn't convinced that he wouldn't meet her.

The elevator doors opened and he stepped forward and into the eyes of Aria.

He stood there for what seemed like minutes, staring into her, not sure of her name anymore. Her eyes were wide, then confused, as she moved out of the elevator and tried to manoeuvre around him.

"Hi," she mumbled, and he stepped aside as she scooted around the corner and disappeared. She was wearing a bathrobe and had a towel slung over one shoulder. Rob stood in the hallway, phone in hand, as the elevator doors shut.

He clicked on the app icon and looked at the message. She still hadn't read it.

A brief thought told him to follow her. But, instead, he pushed the elevator button again and the doors slid open. He entered and leaned back against the steel wall as it carried him upstairs.

Aria bolted down the hallway and into the safety of the changeroom. She was out of breath, and wasn't sure why her heart was banging against her chest. It must have been weeks since she had seen him. She walked into a shower stall and let the water fall over her head and down her body. There was something in the way he looked at her this time around that was different. His eyes were wide. His mouth was open, as if he wanted to say something. As the water soaked her hair, a thought hit her mind. What if he'd finally responded to her message? What if the red flag was his message? Her subscription had already ended and unless she renewed and paid for another six months, there was no way to read her messages. Aria turned off the water and grabbed her towel and robe and headed for the pool. It was too late anyway. She was giving Anthony a chance. He was a good guy. A different guy.

The pool was empty for a change and she slipped into the warm water and began doing laps.

Eighteen

A light snow covered the streets as Rob made his way to the office tower from the subway. His pace was slow and his mind was filled with images of Miranda. The way her eyes glowed when she wanted something. The sounds she made when she was straddled on top of him. And the fire he would face when he saw her in the office. He hadn't responded to her texts last night. She'd sent three more after he didn't respond to the first invitation for drinks. The second was the ignored little girl; the third was the curious lover who was concerned; the last was the woman who refused to be ignored, and that's when he shut off his ringer and went to bed.

What did she want from him? It wasn't love. It was fun—a good rebound fling that he'd needed after Emily. So why did he want to break it off? It would eventually fade on its own.

The concierge greeted him as he walked into the building and stood among the crowd of people as they waited for the next elevator to take them up to their workstations for the day. With six elevators on this side of the building, the wait was always less than a minute, to the benefit of impatient people trying to get to their desk. He wasn't in a hurry, and as the bell rang and the doors opened, Rob turned and headed across the hallway to the entrance to the Tim Horton's. He didn't mind that the line was long but it seemed like less than a minute before the cashier was asking for his order. He wasn't quite certain, his mind filled with other thoughts, but he ordered a coffee and his usual breakfast sandwich. Maybe a donut? No, he decided against it. When the order was placed on the countertop, he didn't stop to make sure it wasn't tea nor did he take his usual sip to make sure there was one sugar and not two.

He rejoined a new crowd at the elevator bank and soon he was riding up to the twenty-fourth floor. When the walls of his cubicle surrounded him, Rob sank into his chair and pressed the button to turn on his computer. He cracked the opening in the coffee lid and took a sip.

"So he is alive. What do you know…?" It was as if the voice spit ice down his back. He didn't want to turn and look, but there was little choice.

"Good morning," he said, turning the chair around. He heard his voice crack and saw one of her eyebrows perk up as she smirked.

"Hi handsome. How was your weekend?" She leaned her body back and perched herself on the edge of his desk, crossing her lean legs in front of him, blocking him from moving forward. She was wearing a short skirt and, despite the fact that it was minus two degrees outside, her legs were bare.

Rob gulped and despite his resistance, he felt aroused.

"I had a pretty good weekend. How about you?"

"I was hoping to see you," she whispered, leaning her face closer to him and uncrossing her legs.

"Oh. I was busy this weekend."

"Busy? On a date?"

"Hey, Miranda, let's not talk about this here," he whispered.

"Okay. My office." Her voice was loud, and she got up, turned, and marched out of his cubicle.

He didn't have to follow her, he told himself later. But she was an executive and he was a middle manager. He got up and walked down the hall, watching her stride on three inches.

She was holding the door handle when he walked in and she shut it as he sat down. The office was a fishbowl so she had positioned her desk so only the side of her face was visible to people walking.

"You didn't respond to my messages," she said. That was Miranda—right to the point.

"Sorry about that. Like I said, I had a busy weekend."

"So you don't have time to send a quick text, to say that you're busy? A few seconds of your busy time?"

Rob had been sent to the principal's office a few times in his school years. He remembered sitting in the seat, feeling tiny compared to the man who sat behind the big desk, leaning over and yelling at him for pulling the fire alarm. He could be arrested, the principal said. The next time it had been for tripping Andy in the playground and making him break his nose when he fell into the side of the swing just as Savitri was pelting forward. Miranda would have made an intimidating principal. But she wasn't his principal and she was not his boss. And this was a personal issue. He leaned forward.

"Look, we were supposed to meet a couple of times and you were a no-show. I'm not interested in games, Miranda."

Her eyes stopped blazing. He was a contender. She sat back in her chair and sighed. "I know. I'm sorry. Things got out of hand around here and, well, I couldn't stop and text. We are in the middle of a really big merger."

The credibility in her voice made Rob feel stupid. She was working. It was a big deal and he was upset because she was late texting him.

"All right. I understand. But we'd already agreed that we should keep our relationship professional."

"I know it wasn't fair, hon, but these days it's tough. And last night, well, I needed a little comfort. I was working all weekend." It's as if she didn't hear the last part of his comment.

Rob still felt like the little kid in the principal's office. He sighed and started to get up from the chair. "All right. I need to get back to work." He didn't want to elaborate. Not at work. In her office.

She leaned forward and smiled. He felt himself relax and sit back down. Then he looked into her eyes. They were glass. This time, he got up without hesitation.

"I have a busy day," he said, before hearing the knock at the door. "Mondays are usually crazy." He didn't realize the CEO was standing outside Miranda's office, on the other side of the glass. The CEO then opened the door enough to ask Miranda to meet him in the meeting room.

Rob smiled at the CEO, who nodded in his direction before turning away. Miranda's face was flushed and she gathered up her computer, before throwing the words "Thank you" in Rob's direction as he walked out of her office and back to his cubicle.

He didn't see her during the day and figured she was in an all-day meeting with the CEO. An issue with the website kept him occupied until just before 7:30, when the office was nearly empty. Two of his staff had families. Siva, a new father who had come from Sri Lanka just three years earlier, bringing a master's degree in IT and a knack for troubleshooting website issues, had to pick up his son at daycare. Melanie, who had two kids in junior school, left promptly at 5 p.m. every day to catch her train to the east end of the city to be home in time for dinner.

It was just Deo and himself left to fix the issues. Siva offered to be available by phone during the evening, but Rob said they could manage. The issue was straightforward enough and by the end of the day, he was fully immersed in the fix.

At 7:30, Rob picked up his coffee cup and headed for the kitchen. Rarely was the place so quiet. The countertop was dotted with dried coffee stains and the coffee urn was a quarter full. Likely old coffee from during the day, he figured, and he dumped the remnants in the sink and was just about to brew a new pot when he realized it was just him. A whole pot of coffee would be wasted unless Deo wanted some.

Rob returned the mug to his cubicle and picked up his wallet. Tim Hortons was always open.

"Hey Deo, I'm going down to Tim's. Want anything?"

The top of a head peeked out from behind his cubicle wall and asked for a tea.

"How about a donut or sandwich? We could be here for another hour or so."

"Do they have beef patties? I'll take one of those."

Rob nodded, and wondered why he thought Deo was a vegetarian. He headed to the elevator that was waiting, doors wide open. Maybe the entire building had already gone home, he thought. As he rode downwards, Rob was aware of the hunger pang in his stomach. He usually ate by 6:00, as soon as he got home, and a beef patty sounded good.

Tim's always had a line no matter the time of day. But the older woman in the hairnet, with the accent, was quick in punching in the order and filling up the beverages. As he stepped to the side to wait for his order, he watched as she attended the next customer. She could have been his own mother, except for the South Asian accent. Did she have kids at home and how did they manage when their mother was working at Tim's in downtown Toronto on a weeknight? His thoughts were interrupted by a paper bag placed in front of him, along with a tray of drinks. He placed the bag on the empty part of the cardboard tray and headed back upstairs with a full tray.

As he stepped off the elevator, the sound of a woman's angry voice made him stop. He listened. Nothing. He was sure he heard some loud whispering, the kind when you're trying to keep your voice low, but the breathing sounds give it away.

He delivered Deo's tea and patty and left the tray on his desk. Walking down the hall to the executive area, Rob heard the sounds of two people talking in hushed tones, the woman sounding upset. Miranda's office was just around the corner.

As he got closer to the end of the hall, just before the left turn to her office, he heard the voice again. It was hers but unlike any tone he'd ever heard come out of her lips in the past. Distraught, crying maybe. Rob couldn't stop walking and as he got to the corner, the CEO's office was visible behind glass walls. Tall plants blocked some of the view but Miranda was recognizable, the CEO's hands around her hips, her face in tears as the older man leaned into her.

Rob felt his anger rise and he couldn't move. He listened but the sounds were lower; the hallway almost quiet. Minutes passed. He moved closer but the sounds were muffled. He wasn't sure how much time passed, but his mind was saying to turn and walk away. There was nothing he could do against the head of the bank. Besides, he had no idea what was going on, and maybe it wasn't his business.

But, instead, he felt his body moving forward and his chest rising with a deep breath. The movement caught the eye of the CEO, who looked up. Rob came out of the shadows and their eyes connected. Like hard magnets refusing to release. The moment hung in the air and Rob felt his fist curl tightly. Suddenly, Miranda turned and Rob's eyes softened as he shifted his gaze to hers. She looked away quickly and Rob took the cue, turned, and walked away.

"Hey Deo, why don't you head out?," he said. "This issue is pretty much resolved. I will continue to monitor it from my computer at home later."

Deo peeked around the corner, an orangey-yellow flake of crust on his lip.

"You sure? I don't mind staying to make sure it's fixed."

"It's getting late. No sense in us sitting here, wasting the night, when I can do it from home." Rob said. He wanted Deo to leave in case the incident moved into view.

He waited about a half an hour before he convinced himself it was time to leave. He pulled on his coat and made his way to the elevator. Rob considered going back down to the executive area to make sure she was all right. But instead, he slipped into the compartment and hit the G button.

As he walked down the street to the subway, the image of Miranda's face was etched in his mind. He had never seen her look so vulnerable.

Nineteen

"So this is date number three?" Mila was painting Aria's toenails.

"Actually, it's four."

"And you haven't had sex yet?"

"Of course not."

"So that's why you want your toes painted. But you know, this colour does not say 'fuck me'. It says, I don't take risks and I'm boring in bed."

Aria shook her head but couldn't help giggling. "Well, I think it's subtly sexy."

"Subtle does not work for men, honey."

"The thing is, I'm not sure if I want to sleep with him yet."

"What?" Mila looked up, the tiny brush suspended in air, and Aria watched as the thick liquid headed towards the tip.

"Mila, it's going to drip…"

"You think I haven't done this before? Now what do you mean you're not sure you want to sleep with him or not? He could move on to someone else if he thinks you're a prude."

"Well, didn't you say that the way he kissed me meant that he likes me and wasn't looking for sex."

Mila swiped the brush on Aria's big toenail. "Yeah, but that was then. Eventually, a man wants to know that you are interested in sex. Have you not heard that women fall in love and then have sex, but men have sex first and then fall in love?"

"Oh yes, I have. It's your mantra," Aria said.

Mila laughed. "It sure is."

Aria had been thinking about Anthony's expectations since he'd asked her to meet for dinner at the pizza place on Roncensvalles. "I hear they make the pizza in a wood-burning oven," he'd said.

She didn't mention that she'd already been there. She suspected that he wanted to be close to her condo, and it was probably time to figure out if they were compatible in bed. Maybe the sex would determine whether they should move forward or not.

When she met Tyler, they'd slept together on the second date and it had just felt natural. A year into their relationship, Aria was making sure the lights were off before she took off her clothes and always put on her robe when she came out of the shower.

The anxiety would envelop her, the fear that he would likely see something that she missed—a pinch of fat, the lack of muscle on her arms. Her body was no longer hers back then. Over time, she'd learned to reclaim it, but now she was protective about who could see it.

What would Anthony think of her body? Aria had made sure that she only ate a quarter of the portions that were placed in front of them at dinner the other night, saying she was full. But the meal had been just as good as the reviews promised and she ignored the nagging of her taste buds that wanted more of the delicate morsels of sliced fish. Instead, she watched Anthony finish the meal and she finished the sake.

"There. You're done. Just prop up those feet for a bit and I'll get us some wine." Mila made her way over to the kitchen, shuffling her feet across the floor in her slippers with the dust mop soles that dusted as she walked. Aria made a note to get a pair, since Mila's floors always looked clean.

"Maybe we should sleep together, just to see..." Aria was thinking out loud.

"To see? Not out of lust?" Mila handed her a wine glass.

"Oh, I'm not convinced that there is lust. Not yet, anyway."

"What? Girl. You are not attracted to him? Doesn't he look like the picture you showed me?"

Aria sighed. "Yeah, he is good-looking and it looks like he works out. But I don't know yet....."

Mila's face softened as she looked over at Aria. "Okay, I get it. He's the first guy since you kicked that scum Tyler to the curb. It's hard to be with someone else. So don't force it. Let it happen naturally."

Aria sipped the wine and felt knots inside her stomach. She wasn't sure what to do.

Mila refused payment as usual and Aria made a note to pick up a bottle of her favourite wine for the next visit. As she waited for the elevator, she ran through the contents of her closet in her mind, wondering what to wear on Wednesday night. A mid-week dinner was a good sign. He didn't want to wait until the weekend. But the logistics of having their first intimate encounter on a weeknight, when the next morning meant getting up early and rushing to get ready for work, were weighing on her. It wasn't practical nor was it romantic. No. She would not sleep with him on Wednesday. They were just having dinner, and if he really liked her, he would wait until the weekend. She would invite him over for a home-cooked meal and get a nice bottle of wine that they could sip over the course of the evening, alone in her apartment.

The ring of the elevator arriving cut through her thoughts and she stepped inside. Her hand hovered on 17 but then changed to G. She might as well check her mail to clean out the junk flyers that must be stuffed inside her mailbox. There were no stops down to the ground floor and when the elevator swung open, Aria stepped out, her mind narrowing down the tops she would wear with her black jeans that had one hole in the knee. Instinct told her to look up just as Rob walked into the other elevator. He didn't see her. She noticed his face was different somehow. A wrinkled forehead or something. The pass-by was too quick. Aria kept walking and didn't look back. It didn't matter.

Rob rode up the elevator, his mind on the CEO's large hands making their way over to Miranda's ass. He was leaning in to kiss her, and she had been crying. So that was the whole issue. She was having an affair with her boss. Or a relationship. Maybe there was no merger.

He flung open the door to his apartment and resisted the urge to throw his laptop bag, placing it on the couch instead. There were two beers left in the fridge and he twisted the cap off one and chugged it. The beef patty was the only food in his stomach, after having eaten it in three bites on the subway, but he wasn't going to make something for dinner. He had no appetite for much else but alcohol.

Rob sat on the couch and activated the Bluetooth app on his phone so he could connect to his speaker. On his music app, he chose Bach's Double Violin Concerto in D Minor, 2nd Movement. His father often played this piece while working behind closed doors in his office. As a young boy, Rob would rap lightly on the door, as his mother had taught him, and wait for his father's voice to give permission to open the door. The sound of the music would waft through the entrance and the room would be filled with the sweetness of the violin. He always felt like he was entering a new world. Like walking through the wardrobe and into Narnia where magic happened and animals talked.

The music was soothing and he ran his hands through his hair. Tanya was thrown back when she found out he listened to Bach. "I wouldn't have guessed," she said. Maybe it was one of the reasons she was drawn to him when they'd met so many years ago.

He sunk into the cushion, leaned back, and sighed. What was he so upset about anyway? They were never really dating. And if Miranda was having a relationship with the CEO, it was none of his business. But she was clearly upset. A quick thought of barging into the office and intercepting the unwelcome exchange entered his mind. But this was the CEO of his company. And Miranda was a strong woman. She could look after herself. Or could she?

He closed his eyes and saw the vision of Miranda's face. Vulnerable, soft. No longer the aggressor that dominated him in bed. Maybe that was the allure. Emily was so passive, unlike Tanya who veered more towards Miranda's style. As the thoughts came together, he realized why he was so fascinated with her. There was danger in dating the corporate lawyer who was miles above his pay grade and, frankly, out of his league. But she wanted him and she wasn't shy about it.

But she was still a woman. Someone who was being dominated herself. Harassed. A powerful man with his hands on the softest part of her body, squeezed up against her so she was unable to move. The near-fear in her eyes drew out the anger inside of him.

Alcohol seeped through his body and Rob picked up his phone. There were flags on the dating app icon, meaning he had messages or smiles or both. He found Miranda's last text and typed. *Hey, are you ok?*

He put the phone back down, sunk back into the couch, and chugged the last of the beer.

Early the next morning, Rob called his team to say he was working from home. Much of his night had been spent monitoring the website issue and checking his phone. Maybe he should have left it alone. Sending her the text meant he was nosing into her business. No wonder she didn't respond.

He showered, put on a pot of coffee, and sat down in front of his computer to start his day.

Twenty

Aria skipped out of work early on Wednesday, using the back door of the office so Margaret wouldn't notice. Her boss wasn't a clock-watcher but Margaret, the administrative assistant who sat near the front entrance, liked to take notes on the times people came and went. And she had favourites. If she saw Aria duck out at 4:00 instead of 5:00, she would position it as a common occurrence, shifting the attention away from Mackenzie, who frequently left the office at 3:00 to catch a yoga class.

Anthony offered to meet at her building so they could walk over together. But she suggested they meet at the pizza place instead. It was only five minutes down the street and the walk would ease her nerves.

Snow crunched under her feet as she headed towards the restaurant. She took careful steps. The soles of her riding boots didn't have the same grip as her hikers, and the recent snowfall camouflaged the ice patches that covered the sidewalks that may or may not have been salted.

The shoemaker's shop was filled with people as usual. The coffee shop on the corner wasn't as fortunate. The businesses on Roncy were frequently changing. A usual occurrence when neighbourhoods are gentrified. Trendy restaurants pop up and work for a short time, but most of their customers were from out of the area, lured by reviews in the paper and visits to the city on Saturday nights. Locals held fast to the cheaper options, keeping their money for high-priced rent and hefty mortgages. Mom-and-pop businesses struggled as the older residents left, making way for millennials and young families who looked for vegan options instead of fried Polish sausages. Eventually, the older residents would be gone, and the ambiance would shift permanently.

The pizza place was one of the few that had been around for years. The owners, an immigrant couple from Italy, used to live in the apartment above the restaurant when the place first opened. Sometimes, they would forget to close the blinds at night, and on mornings, you could see the couple through the large window, making their way down the stairs, sleepy-eyed and ready to start prepping the meals for the lunch hour. The kids would tumble down behind them and fling open the front door to make their way down the street to the public school just off Roncy. That was the rumour that formed over the past twenty years anyway. Aria wasn't around to witness it but the vision was etched into her mind every time she passed the place. Eventually, the family bought a home in Woodbridge after becoming a local hotspot and being written up in the *Toronto Star* as one of the city's best pizza parlours. Their food was consistently good, and prices were relative to most places in Toronto.

Aria opened the door and scanned the room. Three tables were occupied; none with Anthony. She requested a table for two and the hostess began to lead her to the back of the restaurant.

"Can we get one by the window?" she asked.

The hostess grimaced but nodded and put two menus down on the small table near the window by the corner. Aria ordered some water, thinking it would make sense to wait until Anthony arrived before ordering wine. Maybe he'd want to share a half litre.

By 7:07, she had gone through the menu twice and narrowed her options to the one with artichokes and goat cheese, or the one with anchovies and black olives.

"Sorry I'm late. Parking wasn't easy to find." Anthony was taking off his coat as Aria looked up from the menu. He leaned over and she stood halfway, letting him embrace her and touch her cheek with his lips.

"Have you already ordered a drink?" he asked, opening his menu.

"No, I was waiting for you."

"Okay, maybe some wine?"

"Sure, I was thinking half a litre, since a glass is $15 and half a litre is $35. We get about a glass and a half if we order the half litre...I mean, just talking out loud." Aria caught herself and felt her cheeks flush with embarrassment.

Anthony looked up at her and smiled. "Good thinking. I never look at price. You'd think I would, working in banking, but I never think about it."

Aria shifted in her seat and wished she could take back the comments. Why was she always babbling about price? She should've let him decide. Chances are he was paying, so why did she care if he saved a few dollars?

They agreed to share the anchovy pizza and the beet and arugula salad to start. Maybe she would have dessert, she thought, noting that tiramisu was on the dessert list.

"How was your day?" Anthony asked after the waitress

took their order.

"Not bad. But the same old things… meetings, projects, you know."

"Yeah, I hear you. My day was the same. Had some issues with a client, which is why I left the office a bit later than usual."

"Oh? That's too bad. You work downtown, right?"

"Yes."

"Do you commute?"

"Ah, no. I can't abide the subway crammed with people. It takes far too long. Besides, I live in the east end. It's easier to drive."

Aria realized that she had never asked him where he lived. The east end was pretty far from Roncensvalles. Highway driving.

"How is the parking downtown? Is it easy to find a spot?" she asked, conscious of not asking the real question that was on her mind—the cost to park downtown every day.

"It's expensive but I get the monthly pass." He leaned over and reached for her hand. "Ah, but like I said, I never think about money."

Aria didn't ask any more questions, and let him talk about his day and the issue with his client. He told the story well, making her giggle at some points, and she was thankful that she didn't have to talk about her day. Facts about health and how people could take better care of themselves was a topic she wanted to leave at the office.

A few sips of the wine and Aria felt fuzziness in her head, remembering that she had eaten nothing all day except an apple. She was grateful when the salad arrived, and was conscious of chewing slowly, listening to Anthony talk about his upbringing in Scarborough, a continuation of the conversation they had on their first date—Caribbean parents and their misconceptions of Canadian life. Naomi would be pleased with Anthony, and perhaps she was right—sharing the same culture, insights, and understanding was a strong foundation for a relationship. She would no longer have to explain why she didn't speak 'Hindu' and yet was not Black. Why her mother cooked Chinese food and why they celebrated Christmas when they were not Christians. Most of all, the fear, that tiny fear inside her gut, would be gone. The one that surfaced every time they crossed paths with an ethnic person who was a newcomer. Maybe a person wearing a hijab or a turban—white people were never aware of their unconscious biases.

As Anthony spoke about his family, Aria felt more and more relaxed. He could be the right person for her. She could see the two couples on Naomi's father's boat; a sense of belonging and understanding. A feeling of comfort.

"How's your salad?" she finally asked as he paused for a moment.

"Good. Fresh. I love arugula and beets. It's funny how so many people don't like beets. I don't get it. The flavour is so subtle."

"I know. I hear that a lot. Perhaps it's the earthy flavour." Aria couldn't help but smile. They seemed to be on the same page with everything! "I love beets. But I never ate them growing up."

Anthony laughed. "Me either. Caribbean people eat yams and cassava."

"Haha! That is so true." Aria felt warm and leaned back in her chair. "We ate those a lot growing up. My father loves that kind of food. He would get annoyed when my mother cooked potatoes instead of yams or cassava."

"Ah, you know, that kind of food is fattening," Anthony said as he put the last forkful of greens into his mouth and wiped his lip with the napkin to remove a smear of salad dressing.

The word "fattening" hung in the air. Aria said nothing for a couple of seconds. Finally, she managed to respond. "Caribbean food, you mean?"

"Yeah. All of it. Rice and roti and heavy starches like cassava. No wonder Caribbean women tend to be a little on the heavy side. Good thing you started eating beets instead of yams."

He wasn't looking at her when he said it. He was babbling, and taking a drink of wine. Aria speared a beet and placed it in her mouth. There was a bit of greens left on her plate and she forced them down, feeling the urge to excuse herself.

The smell of the pizza arrived before the waitress put it on the table. Anthony served Aria's slice first before taking one himself. He talked about his sister, who gave her toddler Coke in a baby bottle on occasion.

"That kid is going to struggle with weight problems for sure. We keep telling her...my mom and I, but she says it's harmless."

Aria used a knife and fork to cut a thin sliver of pizza and placed it in her mouth. She wanted to gag but forced herself to swallow.

"Hey, are you okay?" Anthony looked genuinely concerned.

"Um, yeah…I'm fine. Do I not seem okay?" She forced a smile.

"Ah. . . you seem upset or something. Not hungry?"

"I, um . . . I don't eat much," she said, lying.

"Women are always watching their weight." He laughed, taking another slice of pizza. "Do you work out?"

"Uh, well I swim a few days per week," she said.

"Ah cool. Swimming is great. I can't say that I'm a strong swimmer but I use the pool in my building sometimes. I actually prefer the hot tub. You know, relaxing with a drink in my water bottle."

She managed to eat the one slice, saying she was full, and he polished off the rest. They chatted about local news while finishing the wine and Anthony asked for the bill, not asking if she wanted dessert.

"Let me help," she said, truly not wanting him to pick it up.

"Nah. Remember what I said?" He winked, putting down his credit card on the table.

He walked her to her condo and stopped at the entrance. He was waiting. Aria wondered if she was overreacting. He'd never said anything about her weight. He was just telling the truth. Caribbean food *was* fattening. She wanted to save the evening. Invite him upstairs for a drink. They would kiss and she would feel better. But nausea was creeping up her throat and she needed to get to the washroom.

"Um, I have an early day tomorrow. It that okay?"

His eyes widened and she watched as disappointment, or maybe surprise, flooded his face. A few seconds later, he recovered with a smile. "Ah sure. I have an early day too. See you on the weekend?"

She nodded, letting him kiss her on the mouth before turning and going back into the building. It was only when she got through the glass doors that she felt tears welling up in her eyes. Somehow, she managed to find the elevators and push the button.

Rob watched the kiss in front of the building. The light from the entrance cast shadows on their faces, but the woman seemed familiar. She was bundled up in a coat, but as he drew closer, he could tell it was her. Aria. The woman from the pool. The one on the dating app that had not responded to his message. He slowed his pace, clutching the bag that held his dinner—burgers from the local place across from the subway. He hadn't eaten all day and was really craving Woody's, but that would've meant going home, grabbing the car, and heading back out. So he'd settled for two smaller ones at the local takeout that was usually busy but had a quick turnover.

The website issue flared up again and the CEO had gone to his boss, saying that the team was incompetent and asking why the manager had worked from home the day before when he knew the website was in a volatile state. As Rob headed into his boss's office to discuss the issue just as the CEO was leaving, neither man averted his eyes and neither smiled as Rob marched past him and closed the door.

Miranda was not around that day. Rob wasn't sure if she was just keeping to herself in the office or if she was away. He passed the CEO in the hallway one more time and saw the man's eyes boring through him, but Rob felt confident and, this time, he nodded as the man stiffened. Protocol forced the head of the company to nod back. Inside, Rob was still angry. Tanya had stories about senior partners using their power to cross boundaries with the young, female lawyers. But he knew that there was nothing he could do unless Miranda filed a formal complaint. If that ever happened, he would step up. He was looking to move on from the bank anyway.

The website issue had taken all day and it was now close to 9pm. Rob's stomach was urging him to get upstairs and tear open the bag. As he hurried towards the condo, he saw Aria and her date and he slowed his pace.

Rob watched the brief kiss and saw the man lean in as if he wanted more. Aria pulled back, the light illuminating her face. Pinched, as if something was troubling her. She turned and seemed to run away from the man and through the glass doors. The man stood at the entrance for a moment, and Rob quickened his pace, as they passed each other on the street. The man was dark-skinned with a silvery stubble on his face. Maybe what a woman would consider good-looking, Rob thought, as he pushed open the door and made his way to the elevator where she was standing. Perhaps aware of his presence, she lifted her head and turned slightly, only to turn away again, bringing her hand up to her face in a wiping motion.

"Hey, are you okay?" Rob heard himself speak.

She turned and looked at him, her eyes watery. "Um, yeah, sorry, I um...nothing, just a bad day." Aria could feel nausea rising.

"Yeah, I hear you. Mine was pretty crappy too," he said, and watched a weak smile flush across her face.

He looked at the numbers above the elevator. One seemed to be stuck on 23. Maybe it was broken. The service elevator was on PH. Someone must be moving in, Rob thought. He hoped, for the first time, that the third one, the one that seemed to be working, would take its time.

Suddenly the doors opened and he felt a pang of disappointment, only to look inside and see that the elevator was full. A man got out and a woman inside the car turned her thumb down to indicate it was heading down.

"Looks like we are in for a wait," he said, and from the corner of her eye, Aria could see that he was looking directly at her. Instinctively, her head turned and they exchanged smiles.

"These elevators are always broken," she said.

"Yeah, they really are. But you know, I have friends who live right downtown and they have the same issues. When elevators are used as much as these ones, they tend to break down." He was babbling but he wanted the conversation to keep going.

"Yeah, I guess that's true." Aria felt herself relax and her breathing slowed. The thoughts of purging became less important.

"Hey, we've met before, right? Aria is it?"

"Yeah, that's right. You're Rob."

"Good memory. I think I saw you in the pool the other day. You're a swimmer. A good one."

"You were watching me?" Aria wasn't sure where the comment came from but it seemed natural. She knew he would smile.

"Well, not really. I mean…I was walking by…" He grinned and she could see the blush on his cheeks.

A sound cut through the air and the elevator doors opened.

"After you," he gestured, and Aria walked inside. The car was empty and no one else was waiting.

He pushed 14 and 17.

"Um, I think we saw each other on the app." She had to say it.

"Yeah, I think so. We may have missed one another." His eyes were suddenly wide, apologetic. "I wasn't a subscriber for a long time, so I couldn't see messages…" his voice trailed off.

"It's okay. I get it." Her eyes were dry, and her stomach calm. The elevator moved. Rob turned to her and said the only thing he could think of to keep the conversation moving.

"Did you have dinner yet? Do you like burgers?"

Acknowledgements

Much thanks to the following for reading, polishing, providing facts, guidance, design and cheers:

Jaclyn Qua-Hiansen
Dave Gregory
Dr. Randy Staab
Roz Milner
Rebecca Rosenblum
Deepa Rajagopalan
Scott Colby
Jordan Sahay
Sohini Ghose
Ellie Hastings
Vanessa Shields

Last but not least, Aimee Parent Dunn for her vision, patience and insight.

Priya Ramsingh is a writer, and photographer. Her debut novel, *Brown Girl in the Room*, was published by Tightrope Books. (2017). Her short story, *Pies for Lunch*, was short-listed for best short fiction in 2021, by *The Caribbean Writer*. She is a former reporter and diversity columnist for *Metroland Media* and continues to write op-eds for the *Toronto Star.* In her spare time, Priya is a wildlife photographer and naturalist. Originally from Trinidad and Tobago, Ramsingh now lives in Toronto.